Thomas Davidson

Prolegomena to In Memoriam

Thomas Davidson

Prolegomena to In Memoriam

ISBN/EAN: 9783337017927

Printed in Europe, USA, Canada, Australia, Japan

Cover: Foto ©Andreas Hilbeck / pixelio.de

More available books at **www.hansebooks.com**

PROLEGOMENA

TO

IN MEMORIAM

BY

THOMAS DAVIDSON

WITH AN INDEX TO THE POEM

S 'io era sol di me quel che creasti
Novellamente, Amor che 'l ciel governi,
Tu 'l sai, che col tuo lume mi levasti.
DANTE

BOSTON AND NEW YORK
HOUGHTON, MIFFLIN AND COMPANY
The Riverside Press, Cambridge
1889

The Riverside Press, Cambridge :
Electrotyped and Printed by H. O. Houghton & Co.

PREFACE.

In writing the following PROLEGOMENA to
In Memoriam, my aim has been to bring out
into clearness the religious soul-problem which
forms its unity. Though I have been familiar
with the poem from boyhood, it is only in the
last few years that the full import of that
problem and of the noble solution offered by
the poet has become clear to me. The work,
as I now understand it, seems to me not only
the greatest English poem of the century, —
which I have always believed, — but one of the
great world-poems, worthy to be placed on the
same list with the *Oresteia*, the *Divina Com-
media*, and *Faust*. If my brief essay contrib-
ute to bring home this conviction to other
persons, I shall feel that I have done them a
service.

The numerous parallel passages which I
have introduced from other writers may per-

haps give my essay a pedantic air. If so, my excuse is this: I wished to show that *In Memoriam* lies in the chief current of the world's thought, since otherwise it would not be a world-poem. For, as George Buchanan says,

> "Sola doctorum monumenta vatum
> Nesciunt Fati imperium severi;
> Sola contemnunt Phlegethonta et Orci
> Jura superbi."

Tennyson is indeed "the heir of all the ages." The roots of his thought have struck down deep into the universal thought, into the Logos.

The INDEX is mainly a copy of one published in 1862 by Moxon & Co., of London. I have merely corrected a few errors, shortened many of the quotations, and adapted the whole to the later editions of the poem. In these there is an additional ode, No. XXXIX. Persons using the Index along with the earlier editions must add one to the number of every ode after the thirty-eighth.

THOMAS DAVIDSON.

NEW YORK, *February 13, 1889.*

CONTENTS.

————◆————

PROLEGOMENA TO IN MEMORIAM.

INTRODUCTION.

PROLOGUE.

The Decay and Restoration of Faith. The Nature of Faith and its Relation to Understanding.

OUT of original character, instruction, and experience every human being builds up his own moral world, an ideal order of things which imparts to his actions whatever rationality and aim they may possess. Upon the world thus created everything in his life depends, his optimism or pessimism, his happiness or misery. If his world is rational, inspiring faith and courage, by offering motives for continuous, enthusiastic activity, his life, whatever may befall, is a blessed unity. If, on the contrary, his world fails to disclose any purpose, any reason why one course of action should be preferred to another, anything worthy of supreme love and devotion, life is fragmentary, feeble, and, when temperament fails, miserable. Success in life, in the deepest sense, depends upon his power to build up and sustain an aimful and consistent moral world.

Unfortunately, such a world, even after it has been built up, may be destroyed, and no greater disaster can happen to any man.[1] In such an event, the will is paralyzed, and life loses meaning and direction.[2] And, since a man's moral world is the response to his whole moral nature, including three elements, insight, love, and energy, the catastrophe may come through the failure of any one of these, that is, through doubt, widowed or blasted affection, or unavailing activity. The world of a Faust is shattered by the first, that of a Tennyson by the second, that of a Charles Albert by the third.

A shattered moral world means a world without rationality or aim. Now the postulates of the reason, as Kant has shown, are God, Freedom, Immortality. Let a man doubt whether there be any moral law in the world, whether he be free to obey such law, or whether obedience to that law will result in good, and disobedience in evil, to him, and his moral world is wrecked. Life, offering no motive for moral action, is not worth living.

In Memoriam is the record of the shattering and rebuilding of a moral world in a man's

---

[1] Admirably brought out in Frances Browne's *Losses.*
[2] As Tennyson puts it (*In Mem.,* iv. 1),

> " My will is bondsman to the dark;
> I sit within a helmless bark."

soul. It belongs to the same class of works as the *Divine Comedy* and *Faust;* only, whereas the first of these, despite its title, is epic, and the second dramatic, this is lyric. The hero of *In Memoriam*, like the hero of the *Divine Comedy*, is the poet himself. Both poems are idealized records of actual experiences. In both the person beloved dies young, leaving the lover for a time utterly desolate. In both cases this desolation, instead of overwhelming the lover, finally quickens his spiritual perceptions, so that he is enabled to find in the spiritual world what he has lost in the material one, to recover in incorruption what he has lost in corruption. In both cases, a pure, reverent human love leads the soul of the lover up to God. Tennyson's Arthur does for the deeply religious and cultivated man of the nineteenth century what Dante's Beatrice did for the similarly endowed man of the fourteenth. Dante finds again his lost Beatrice in the imaginary paradise of his time; Tennyson finds his Arthur "mix'd with God and Nature." In both poems, the *Divine Comedy* and *In Memoriam*, the fundamental thought is the same: Man's true happiness consists in the perfect conformity of his will to the divine will, and this conformity is attained through love, first of man, and then of God. "Our wills are ours to make them thine" is the modern rendering of "E la sua voluntade è nostra pace."[1]

In Memoriam naturally suggests the Platonic Sonnets of Shakespeare (I.–CXXVI.); but there is really no more than a most superficial resemblance between the two works, due to the fact that both are addressed by one man to another. In Shakespeare's Sonnets there is no rising from flesh to spirit, only a series of love-vicissitudes. The truth is, *In Memoriam* bears about the same relation to Shakespeare's Sonnets as the *Divine Comedy* does to Petrarch's.

In *In Memoriam* the poet's moral world is shattered by widowed affection, by the loss of a beloved friend, in whom he had found that brother, that more-than-brother,[2] through whose lovableness he was able to comprehend the divine lovableness,[3] in a word, to see God.[4]

[1] *Paradise*, iii. 85. Compare the last lines of the poem.

[2] "More than my brothers are to me," ix. 5; lxxix. 1.

[3] He that loveth not his brother whom he hath seen, cannot love God whom he hath not seen.—1 John iv. 21.

[4] "The expression of an eye,
Where God and Nature met in light." (cxi. 5.)

"Though mix'd with God and Nature thou,
I seem to love thee more and more." (cxxx. 3.)

Cf. what Dante says of Beatrice (*Vita Nuova*, cap. xxvi.).

"Ella sen va, sentendosi laudare,
Benignamente d' umiltà vestuta;

This loss and the ensuing grief and darkness of soul raised in the poet's mind doubts with regard to the righteousness or moral government of the world, and robbed life of its meaning. The poem describes in detail the nature of these doubts, and the process by which they were ultimately dispelled, and faith in God, Freedom, and Immortality was restored.

The philosophic meaning of the poem is summed up in the prologue, written in 1849. This takes the form of an address or prayer to "immortal Love," the "strong Son of God," the author of all things in heaven and in earth, of life and of death, the source of that justice which makes life rational. Tennyson, like Dante,[1] holds that the efficient cause of the universe is love, and that life without love is worse than death.[2] Nor is the divine love

> E par che sia una cosa venuta
> Di cielo in terra a miracol mostrare,"

and what Emerson says to his friend in "Friendship":

> "Through thee alone the sky is arched,
> Through thee the rose is red.
> All things through thee take nobler form,
> And look beyond the earth;
> The mill-round of our fate appears
> A sun-path in thy worth."

[1] "L'amor che muove il sole e l'altre stelle." *Parad.*, last line.

[2] See xxvi. 3, 4. Compare Aristotle's words: "Without friends no one would choose to live, though he possessed all other good things." *Nik. Eth.*, viii. 1 : 1155*a*,

which made and sustains the universe different in kind from human love.

> " Thou seemest human and divine,
> The highest, holiest, manhood, thou."

We may, therefore, trust the divine love for all
that we should expect from the highest human
love, and more. The universe will satisfy the
three postulates of the reason.

(1.) It will be governed by a moral law far
more perfect than any that can be expressed
in human systems.

> " Our little systems have their day ;
> They have their day and cease to be :
> They are but broken lights of thee,
> And thou, O Lord, art more than they." [1]

5 *sq.* Also Fichte's : " Life is love ; and the whole form
and force of life consist in love, and arise out of love."
Way to a Blessed Life, Lect. i. This doctrine may be
said to be fundamental in Aryan thought. The Veda
tells us, speaking of creation : —

> " Then first came Love upon it, the new spring
> Of mind — yea, poets in their hearts discerned,
> Pondering, this bond between created things
> And uncreated."

Hesiod makes Love ('Epws) the child of Chaos and the
brother of Earth (*Theog.*, 120) ; and Parmenides, speaking of Genesis, says : —

" Foremost of gods she gave birth unto Love ; yea, foremost of all
gods."

See Plato, *Sympos.*, 178 B. And who does not remember
the glorious address to Venus, as the author of all life,
in the exordium of Lucretius' poem ?

[1] Compare the words uttered by Hêrakleitos, five

(2.) It will leave the human will free, even though reason may be unable to see how; but that freedom will be secured only by conformity to the divine will.

> "Our wills are ours, we know not how; ·
> Our wills are ours, to make them thine."[1]

(3.) It will make possible a conscious immortality for the individual. Our sense of justice demands this.

> "Thou wilt not leave us in the dust:
> Thou madest man, he knows not why;
> He thinks he was not made to die;
> And thou hast made him: thou art just."

But all these things, the poet admits, are only postulates of reason, matters of faith, not objects of understanding or knowledge.

> "We have but faith: we cannot know;
> For knowledge is of things we see;
> And yet we trust it comes from thee,
> A beam in darkness: let it grow."

This verse contains the whole gist of the

hundred years before our era: "All human laws are fed by one, the divine. For it prevaileth as far as it listeth, and sufficeth for all, and surviveth all." (Frag., xci. edit. Bywater.)

---

[1] Cf. "Anzi è formale ad esto beato esse
Tenersi dentro alla divina voglia,
Perch' una fansi nostre voglie stesse.

. . . .

E la sua voluntade è nostra pace."
Divina Commed., Parad., iii. 79 *sqq.*

poem, which might very well have for its second title, "'The Decay and Revival of Faith." Since, then, faith is the source of all those convictions which give life its meaning, we must here stop and carefully inquire : What is faith? How does it stand related to knowledge? What are its credentials? These are all one question under different aspects.

Faith (πίστις), as a philosophic term, seems to have been first employed by Parmenides. It occurs in his extant fragments twice, and each time means direct intellectual intuition of necessary truth, as opposed to mere contingent opinion, arrived at through the medium of sensuous experience or moral persuasion.

The passages are these : —

(1)   "Thou needs must investigate all things,
First the errorless core of the truth that lightly persuadeth,
Then the opinions of mortals, where no true *faith* doth inhabit "

(2) " Ne'er will the potence of *faith* admit that from being proceedeth
Aught but itself."

Faith, then, according to Parmenides, instead of being something inferior to empirical knowledge, which " is of things we see," is superior to it, being the very "errorless core of the truth," the necessary assent given by the mind to what is self-evident. By the time of Aristotle faith has lost this lofty position, as the source of certainty, and come to mean the assent which the mind, not by necessity of evidence, but by the balancing of probabilities, accords to the conclusions of experience. "Faith follows opinion,"[1] says that philosopher. From this time on, in Greek thought, the term wavers between these two meanings, intuition and belief. Proklos, the last of the great Greek thinkers, holds faith to be the highest of the three ways leading to God, the other two being love and truth. It is due to direct divine illumination. Some Christian sects held the same doctrine; but, in the Christian world, faith had early many different meanings. F. C. Baur enumerates six senses in which it is used by St. Paul.[2] In the Epistle to the Hebrews we read, "Faith is the substance of the things hoped for, the test of the things that are not seen." In modern philosophical language this would read: Faith is the immediate intuition of the ideal, as distinct from the real, world. St. Augustine defines faith as "thinking with assent,"[3] and Thomas Aquinas, agreeing with this, says: "The act which is believing includes a firm adherence

---

[1] Δόξη ἔπεται πίστις, *De An.*, iii. 3: 428a 20

[2] *Vorlesungen über neutestamentliche Theologie*, p. 154.

[3] Credere est cum assensione cogitare. *De Prædestinatione Sanctorum*, chap. ii., on which see Thomas Aquinas, *Sum. Theolog.*, II.[2], q. ij. art. 1.

to one side (of a question), and in so far the believer coincides with the knower and under-stander; and yet his knowledge is not perfect through clear vision, and in so far he agrees with the doubter, the suspecter, and the opiner. And thus it is characteristic of the believer that he thinks with assent. For this reason, this act of belief is distinguished from all other acts of the intellect that relate to the true and the false." . . . " The intellect of the believer is determined to one alternative, not by reason, but by will." Among modern theo-logians no one has dealt so explicitly with faith as Rosmini, who gives the following as the order of the acts of the soul which pre-cede, constitute, and follow the act of faith.

"(1.) Revealed knowledge of God, through hearing (external action).

"(2.) Perception of God, or effectual light is-suing from that revealed knowledge, especially from that part of it which is mysterious (action performed in the essence of the soul).

"(3.) A consequent feeling, a sweet and sub-lime delight, issuing from that perception, and persuading us of the truth of the things per-ceived.

"(4.) Power to believe and act holily, the effect of this feeling.

"(5.) Voluntary act of belief, a practical judgment on the truth and excellence of the things known and perceived, an act of estimation, the recognition of God as light, truth, and infinite authority. This act, if a man does not recalcitrate with his evil will, is followed by love and holy, meritorious acts of living faith.

"(6.) Love, which follows this act of practical estimation.

"(7.) Holy action, following from love."[1]

M. Renan, speaking of the question of individual immortality, says: "Perhaps it is well that an eternal veil should cover truths which have a value only when they are the fruit of a pure heart."[2] The implication here is that it is purity of heart that gives eyes to faith. " Blessed are the pure in heart, for they shall see God."

Such are a few of the attempts made by great and profoundly religious men, from the rise of philosophy to the present day, to give a meaning to the word ' faith.' Though showing wide differences in results, they agree in two things: (1) That faith is a faculty of the soul which enables it to grasp truths inaccessible to understanding and knowledge, the very truths which are required to give life its meaning and consecration; (2) that its efficacy depends upon a condition of the heart and will, upon a pure heart and a good will.

[1] *Antropologia Soprannaturale*, pp. 94 *sq.*
[2] Introduction to the *Book of Job*.

It is these two essential elements that enter into Tennyson's conception of faith.   Faith gives us

> " truths that never can be proved
> Until we close with all we loved,
> And all we flow from, soul in soul." [1]

It "comes of self control;"[2] it has its source in reverence;[3] it is the protest of the heart against the " freezing reason's colder part." It is wisdom, as distinct from, and superior to, knowledge.   That the poet identifies faith with wisdom is clear from a comparison of the following passages :

> " Let knowledge grow from more to more,
> But more of reverence in us dwell;
> That *mind* and *soul*, according well,
> May make one music as before,

> " But vaster."

> " For she (knowledge) is earthly of the *mind,*-
> But Wisdom heavenly of the *soul.*"

Here Wisdom is written with a capital, to show that it means the personified wisdom of the Alexandrine Jews, which was another name for the Logos, or Word, spoken of in the opening verses of St. John's Gospel, and identified with Christ.[4]   But, though faith or wisdom deals

---

[1] cxxxi. 3; Cf. Prol., 1, 6; lv. 5; cxxiv. 6; cxxvii. 1.
[2] cxxxi. 3.
[3] Prol., 7 ; cxiv. 6.
[4] See *Proverbs,* iii. 19; viii., ix., and the whole *Book*

with higher things than knowledge does, it is inferior to knowledge in power to produce certainty. The reason of this is that its objects are formless, and the human mind has difficulty in thinking anything of this sort. "We walk by faith, not by form,"[1] says St. Paul. But, as Aristotle remarks, "The soul never thinks without a phantasm."[2] Hence, we are compelled, in order to grasp the things of faith, to have them presented to us in the form of a parable, allegory, myth, or tale. As Dante so well says (*Parad.*, iv. 40):

> " Thus it behoves your minds to be addressed,
> Because alone from things of sense they seize,
> What then they render fit for intellect.
>   And so it is that Scripture condescends
> To your ability; and hands and feet
> Ascribes to God, and meaneth something else."

Tennyson often insists upon the necessity of a form for faith, for example :

> " O thou that after toil and storm
>   Mayst seem to have reach'd a purer air,
>   Whose *faith* has centre everywhere,
> Nor cares to fix itself to *form*,

of Wisdom, perhaps written by Philo the Jew, whose works contain much regarding Wisdom and the Logos. Cf. 1 Corinth. i. 30.

[1] 2 Corinth. v. 7. Such is the correct translation of this passage. Cf. The figure of this world passeth away. 1 Corinth. vii. 31.

[2] *De Anima*, iii. 7 : 431*a* 16 *sq.*

" Leave thou thy sister when she prays.

.   .   .   .

" Her *faith* thro' *form* is pure as thine." [1]

" And all is well, though *faith* and *form*
Be sundered in the night of fear." [2]

" Though *truths* in manhood darkly join
Deep-seated in our mystic frame,
We yield all blessing to the name
Of Him that made them *current coin.*

" For *Wisdom* dealt with mortal powers
Where *truth in closest words* shall fail,
When *truth embodied in a tale*
Shall enter in at lowly doors." [3]

This last quotation helps us to understand
the relation of faith to knowledge, and to find
the credentials for the former. The truths of
faith are contained in our very frame or constitution, which is mystical, that is, opens out
into the Infinite, into God. Every soul can
truly say, "I and the Father are one." Tennyson often dwells upon this mystic union of the
finite with the Infinite. Speaking of the origin
of the individual soul, he says :

" A soul shall draw from out the vast
And strike his being into bounds,

" And, moved thro' life of lower phase,
Result in man, be born and think." [4]

[1] xxxiii. 1, 3.   [2] cxxvii. 1.
[3] xxxvi. 1, 2.   [4] Epilogue, 31.

Of the birth of the individual consciousness, he says :

> " But as he grows he gathers much
> And learns the use of ' I ' and 'me,'
> And finds ' I am not what I see,
> And other than the things I touch.'

> " So rounds he to a separate mind
> From whence clear memory may begin,
> As thro' the frame that binds him in
> His isolation grows defined."

Other even more distinct utterances to the same effect may be found in the poems, " Flower in the crannied wall," " De Profundis," and "The Higher Pantheism," in the last of which occur these verses :

" Dark is the world to thee: thyself art the reason why:
For is He not all but thou, that hast power to feel ' I
am I !'

" Glory about thee, without thee : and thou fulfillest thy
doom,
Making Him broken gleams, and a stifled splendor and
gloom.

" Speak to Him thou, for He hears, and Spirit with
Spirit can meet —
Closer is He than breathing, and nearer than hands and
feet."

The gist of all this is, that the human being, in putting on individuality, in striking his being into bounds, in rounding to a separate mind capable of knowledge, readily loses the consciousness of his oneness with the Infinite,[1] which consciousness is faith, the condition of all knowledge, as Parmenides saw. St. Bonaventura has put this admirably :

"Strange is the blindness of the intellect which does not consider that which it first sees, and without which it can know nothing. But, as the eye, when intent upon the variety of colors, does not see the light through which it sees other things, or, if it sees, does not observe it, so the eye of our mind, when intent upon these particular and universal entities, does not observe that being which is above all genus, although it is first presented to the mind, and all other things are presented only through it. Whence it is most truly manifest that, as the eye of the bat behaves to the light, so the eye of our mind behaves to the most obvious things of nature.[2] The reason is, that,

---

[1] Compare Wordsworth, "Our birth is but a sleep and a forgetting" (*Ode to Immortality*), and Mrs. Browning's lines near the beginning of *Aurora Leigh* :

> " I have not so far left the coasts of life
> To travel inland, that I cannot hear
> The murmur of the outer Infinite,
> Which unweaned babies smile at in their sleep,
> When wondered at for smiling."

[2] This sentence is almost a literal translation from Aristotle, who is not usually regarded as mystical: "Ὥσπερ γὰρ τὰ τῶν νυκτερίδων ὄμματα πρὸς τὸ φέγγος ἔχει τὸ μεθ' ἡμέραν, οὕτω καὶ τῆς ἡμετέρας ψυχῆς ὁ νοῦς πρὸς τὰ τῇ φύσει φανερώτατα πάντων (the things most obvious in their nature). *Metaph.*, Λ², 1 : 993*b* 9 *sqq.*

being accustomed to the darkness of (individual) objects, and the phantasms of sensible things, when it sees the light of the highest being, it seems to see nothing (not understanding that this very darkness is the highest illumination of our minds); just as when the eye sees pure light, it seems to see nothing." [1]

But, while our "isolation" through the flesh obscures for us our oneness with the Infinite, it serves to define our individual personality :

> " This use may lie in blood and breath,
>   Which else were fruitless of their due,
>   Had man to learn himself anew
> Beyond the second birth of Death." [2]

And even when the flesh falls away, and we

> "close with all we loved
> And all we flow from, soul in soul," [3]

this individuality will continue :

> " Eternal form shall still divide
>   The eternal soul from all beside." [4]

From all this it is clear that, while knowledge is the consciousness of our distinctness from the Infinite, and the relation of our spirits, as distinct, to it, faith is the consciousness of our oneness with the Infinite. It is in this double consciousness that the essence of religion and man's true blessedness consist.

---

[1] *Itinerarium Mentis in Deum*, chap. v.

[2] xlv. 4.   [3] cxxxi. 3.   [4] xlvii. 2.

The human spirit shrinks from the thought of losing either side of it, of losing knowledge of self and not-self, and sinking into a Buddhistic *nirvâna*, or of losing faith, and finding itself an unsustained, hopeless wanderer in an alien universe. And all causes for such shrinking arise from the difficulty of finding symbols or forms in which to express and justify the content of faith to knowledge, in which alone there is perfect clearness for the ordinary man. All religions have been merely so many attempts to find such symbols [1] or forms, and their success has depended upon the fitness of these. The fit symbol is that which finds a response, an "assent," as Augustine and Thomas Aquinas call it, in the faculty of faith, which Tennyson, following an old usage, calls the soul,[2] or heart,[3] as distinct from mind,[2] or reason,[3] — the faculty of knowledge. Now, the question with regard to the credentials of faith resolves itself into an inquiry into the nature and validity of this response or assent, and this, again, leads us to consider the nature of assent in general.

[1] Symbol is the Greek word for creed, as well as for the signs in the sacraments.

[2]   "That *mind* and *soul*, according well,
        May make one music as before." (Prol., 7.)

[3] "A warmth within the breast would melt
        The freezing *reason's* colder part,
        And, like a man in wrath, the *heart*
        Stood up and answered, 'I have felt.'" (cxxiv. 4.)

What, then, is assent? As no one has dealt with this question so fully as Rosmini, we may answer in his words: "Assent is the act by which a man voluntarily affirms with subjective efficacy any object which is present to his intelligence," such object being always a possible or ideal judgment. To understand a proposition and to assent to it are two widely different things. The mere fact that I understand the proposition. " The soul is immortal," does not compel me to give my assent to it. What, then, is it in a proposition that compels assent? The feeling or consciousness that, if we withheld assent, we should be doing violence to our own nature. I cannot, for example, refuse my assent to the proposition, " Not more than one straight line can be drawn through a given point, parallel to another straight line," or to this, " Nothing can act before it is," without doing violence to my rational powers, and destroying the very possibility of truth. And I have much the same feeling when I refuse assent to the propositions, " My will is free," " My soul is immortal," " My actions have inevitable and eternal consequences to me." I feel that, if these are not true, there is no meaning in anything ; my existence and all existence is irrational, mere vanity of vanities. It is true that Kant has tried to show that the assent which we give to propositions in mathematics and philosophy of nature has grounds such as are altogether wanting to the assent which we may accord to metaphysical propositions. He says that in the first case we are aided by time and space, the forms of sense, and in the second by the categories of the understanding,[1] whereas, when we come to the last, we find in the "pure reason" no form or forms enabling us to have experience of its objects, and so can only assume them as postulates, without ever being able to say whether in reality anything corresponds to them. But is Kant right in this? Is it true that the pure reason has no forms making experience of its objects possible? Was not Parmenides, the ancient Kant, right, when he said, in his poetical way, that Justice (Δίκη) was the teacher of the highest truth?[2] And are not the oft-repeated words of the Bible true: "The just shall live by faith"?[3] Is not justice the form of the 'pure reason,' of that higher consciousness which we call faith? Is it not true that just as all sensuous apprehension is conditioned by space and time, and all

---

[1] These Schopenhauer has very correctly reduced to the one category of Cause or Causation.

[2] There are few things in literature finer than his account of how he was led to Truth by Justice. See my translation of his Fragments, *Journal of Speculative Philosophy*, vol. iv. pp. 1–16.

[3] Habb. ii. 4; Rom. i. 17; Gal. iii. 11; Heb. x. 38, etc.

understanding by cause, so all 'pure reason,' or faith (πίστις), is conditioned by justice or righteousness, taken in its broadest sense? And was not Kant forced virtually to admit this, when he came to treat of ethics? Is not his 'categorical imperative:' 'Act so that the maxim of thy will may be accepted as the principle of universal legislation,' — a mere awkward way of saying, " Justice is the law of the universe "? And, in spite of this awkwardness, does not Kant find that his maxim involves three moral postulates — Freedom, Immortality, God? The fact is that Kant, failing to see that justice is the form of the pure reason, which is essentially moral, left the form of morality a mere blind imperative, and invented a spurious faculty, the practical reason, to deal with it. As a consequence, he was compelled to leave the facts which justice interprets to consciousness mere postulates. Let us once realize that justice is the form of reason, and these facts will present themselves as real. We shall then find the law of justice as necessary and universal as the law of cause; and God will be no longer a postulate, but the supreme reality. This reality is moral in its nature, and can be reached only through the moral faculty, which is the pure reason,[1] or

[1] On the error of assuming a practical reason, see Rosmini, Introduction to *Principles of Moral Science.*

faith, in its original sense. This being true, all propositions explicating the form of faith ought to command our assent as readily as those explicating the forms of sense and understanding. For example, the proposition, "The human will is free," should command it as certainly as, "Not more than one straight line can be drawn through a given point parallel to another straight line," or, "Nothing can act before it is."

But it will be said, We cannot help assenting to the last two : nobody ever doubted them ; whereas we are by no means forced to assent to the first. The most obvious reply to this is, that the last two propositions have both been frequently not only doubted, but denied. Many modern geometers have denied the first ;[1] Spinoza and Fichte denied the second.[2] But, after all, it is true that the propositions of pure reason are doubted and denied much more frequently than those of sense and understanding ; that they do not so readily command assent as these. There must be some reason for this. Let us consider it.

When we observe that the propositions de-

[1] See Stallo's *Concepts and Theories of Modern Physics*, pp. 207 *sqq.*; chap. xiii.

[2] Spinoza's *Causa sui*, which plays so prominent a part in his system, involves this denial, and Fichte's assertion that "the *Ego* originally absolutely posits its own being" openly expresses it.

pending upon the forms of sense are less frequently denied than those depending upon the form of the understanding, and this because the former are more easy to grasp completely than the latter, we ought to expect that the latter would be less frequently denied than those depending upon the form of faith. But there is another and deeper reason for the latter fact. The faculty of faith is much more easily deranged and impaired in its activity than that of understanding, and requires more careful training. It is dependent upon the life which a man leads, and acts normally only in the man whose life is free from stain. " If any one do His will, he will know of the doctrine, whether it be of God." The assent which the soul gives to the propositions of faith is a moral assent, accorded by the moral faculty, which cannot judge correctly, unless it has built up for itself a moral world, by righteous action. Each human being has his own world, built up through his own faculties. His sensuous world is built up through sense and its forms ; his intelligible world through understanding and its form ; his moral world through faith and its form — justice. If a man has built up no moral world for himself by just action, how can he discover the principle of that world, the absolute Justice, or God, or how can he find a fit symbol for the

same in either understanding or sense? There
is no knowledge without experience.

There is a third reason why the assent of
the mind is given with some hesitancy to the
objects of faith, and this is, because for ages
this assent has been demanded, and under
wrong influences given, to many propositions
that are not based upon justice at all, but
upon mere fancy and credulity. In rejecting
these propositions, the reason has also re-
jected those that are founded on justice. As
in every case, by forcing a faculty to do something unnatural, we have unfitted it for per-
forming its proper function. In attempting to
believe myths, we have ceased to be able to
believe the truth. But, as Lowell says, "the
soul is still oracular," and when its deeds are
pure, it will find fitting symbols for the Infinite
Justice.

The result of all these drawbacks is, that
the moral assent, which, conditioned by justice, affirms God, Freedom, and Immortality, is
given feebly and falteringly, and, in hours of
spiritual darkness, withheld altogether. Hence
Tennyson calls upon his friend to be near him
when his "light is low," and when his "faith
is dry," and, at the very last, he speaks of the
objects of faith as "truths that never can be
proved," until men return to the bosom of
God. This only means that the poet, not re-

garding the response of the moral nature, whose form is justice, as final and sufficient, looks for a response from the understanding, to which the things of reason can appear only in the form of symbols, or, as Henry George so admirably puts it, "a shadowy gleam of ultimate relations, the endeavor to express which inevitably falls into type and allegory." But such a response can never be given, in this world or any other; for the response of the soul to the Infinite Justice is not commanded by knowledge, but by blessedness. Dante knows that he has seen God only because, in saying so, he feels that he is filled with larger bliss.[1] We are mistaken when we think that understanding is the highest faculty of the soul, or certifies to the deepest realities. Above it is that faculty which the understanding cannot even define, but which it compares to the confidence reposed in a true and tried friend and calls faith, and which is the human reflex of the Divine Wisdom, man's consciousness of the Infinite and his oneness therewith.

---

[1] " La forma universal di questo nodo
Credo ch' io vidi, perchè più di largo,
Dicendo questo, mi sento ch' io godo.''
Parad., xxxiii. 91 *sqq.*

CHAPTER I.

(i–viii.)

The poet justifies his grief, describes its effects, explains why he writes of it, refuses cheap consolation, and seeks only to embalm the past.

THE earliest expression which Tennyson gave to his grief for the loss of his friend is the exquisite lyric, "Break, break, break," in which he makes us feel that his soul is utterly out of harmony with the world, that its light is gone, that only darkness and despair are left.

In Memoriam opens in a somewhat less despairing tone. Numb, voiceless grief has given place to sorrow mingled with reflection. The poet finds it necessary even to justify his grief to himself. He might, by treading down his past self, that moral world I. whose light was his friend, rise to higher things. He formerly believed such a course possible; but now he cannot realize it. The world of his past is the only one wherein his soul is at home. Better a world with love clasping grief than a world without love. The constancy of our love is the measure of our worth.

But sorrow is deadening. In clinging to his
II.   dead past, he feels like the yew tree
that grasps at tombstones. "whose
fibres knit the dreamless head " below. A
"thousand years of gloom " have settled on
him, and in that gloom, Sorrow whispers des-
olating doubts. suggesting that the
III.   whole universe may be a mere mockery, "signifying nothing." Such doubts para-
lyze the will, and send all the powers
IV.   to sleep. The poet sits "within a
helmless bark"; his life has lost direction.
His very heart beats sluggishly for want of desire or motive. and he scarcely has courage to
ask why, or warmth to melt the tears that have
frozen at their springs. Only at morning the
will shows a little strength, and struggles not
to be "the fool of loss." He then seeks to
relieve his torpor by putting his grief in words;
but this seems almost a sin, all words
V.   are so superficial and inadequate.
Still. since the "sad mechanic exercise " of
writing verses acts like a narcotic, "numbing
pain," he will go on writing, in order to shield
himself from cold despair. This method of
numbing pain is, indeed, his only refuge; acceptance is out of the question. Friends try
to console him by reminding him
VI.   that "loss is common to the race";
but such comfort is mere chaff. The common-

ness of loss does not make it less bitter in any one case. The pathos, the awfulness, the surprise of death remain forever the same. Nothing can fill the blank made by the loss of the beloved friend. So the poet turns back to the now darkened world of the past, VII. visits the scenes where he and his friend have been happy together, and finds a little comfort in continuing the art of poetry which they had cultivated in VIII. common, and in consecrating it to the memory of the departed. Its chief worth now is that it pleased him, and serves to embalm his memory.

CHAPTER II.

(ix–xxi.)

The circumstances of the friend's death, the return of the body to England, and its burial.

AFTER the alleviation derived from writing
verses to the memory of his friend,
the next thing that comforts the poet
is the return of the friend's body to England
and its burial in English soil. He prays for
every blessing upon the ship that bears his
"lost Arthur's loved remains." In imagination
he follows it day and night on
its voyage, like a guardian angel, lest
anything should befall it, and the remains be
lost. Under the influence of the
soothing autumn weather, he feels a
certain calm ; but it is only the calm of despair,[1]
and even that does not last. Impatience
drives him to meet the ship,
which brings but death instead of life, cause
for tears instead of for joy. So strange is it

IX.

X.

XI.

XII.

---

[1] Compare the lines of Burns :

"Come, Autumn, sae pensive in yellow and grey,
And soothe me wi' tidings o' nature's decay ;
The dark, dreary winter an' wild drivin' sna'
Alane can delight me — my Nannie 's awa."

that the body should return without the in-
forming spirit, that he seems to "suf-
fer in a dream," so that his "eyes   XIII.
have leisure for their tears," and his fancy
for play. But, if the ship should
bring the living instead of the dead   XIV.
friend, he would not be surprised, so little has
he yet realized the thought of his
death. The approach of tempestu-   XV.
ous winter changes the "calm despair" of
the poet's soul into a "wild unrest," which
would be overwhelming, were it not for the
fancy that the ship bearing his friend's body
is peacefully sailing "athwart a plane of
molten glass." Such change from
one extreme to the other seems sur-   XVI.
prising, and the poet can account for it only
by supposing that it is unreal, or else that sorrow has utterly unhinged him, stunned him,
and made him delirious. In any case, life has
become confused and purposeless. At last the
ship arrives, bringing the remains in safety,
and the poet once more prays for
every blessing henceforth to accom-   XVII.
pany it for such kind service. Then the funeral takes place. Hallam is buried in
Clevedon church, in Somersetshire;   XVIII.
in a "still and sequestered situation, on a lone
hill that overhangs the Bristol Chan-
nel," "and in the hearing of the   XIX.

wave."[1]   This brings the mourner some slight comfort.

> "'Tis well; 'tis something; we may stand
>   Where he in English earth is laid,
>   And from his ashes may be made
> The violet of his native land."

His grief now ebbs and flows, like the tides; it is no longer a changeless flood.   During the ebbs — which bear the same relation to the flows as the grief of servants to that of chil-

XX.

dren in a house "where lies the master newly dead "— he can speak.   At other times, the words die on his lips, for grief that may not be spoken.   Such grief the world does not understand, but looks upon as mere

XXI.

subtle vanity, as waste of energy that might be employed in some practical or scientific pursuit, which alone it can appreciate.   The poet can only reply:

> "Behold, ye speak an idle thing:
>   Ye never knew the sacred dust:
>   I do but sing because I must,
> And pipe but as the linnets sing."[2]

[1] The funeral took place on 3d January, 1834, the death on the 15th September previous.

[2] Compare Goethe's lines:

> " Ich singe, wie der Vogel singt
>   Der in den Zweigen wohnet;
>   Das Lied, das aus der Kehle dringt,
>   Ist Lohn, der reichlich lohnet."
>   *Meister's Lehrjahre*, II. ii.

CHAPTER III.

(xxii–xxvii.)

The friendship for the dead. Its reality and blessedness. Not to be quenched by time or sorrow.

YEA, the poet has good cause to mourn. His loss is incalculable. The friend- **XXII.** ship so rudely interrupted by death was the very light of his life for four years, years full of pure happiness and lofty endeavor. Between these and the **XXIII.** darkened present what a contrast! And here a question arises in the poet's mind, whether it is not just this contrast **XXIV.** that makes the years of friendship seem so perfect; but his consciousness an- swers promptly and affirms, "I know **XXV.** that this was Life"; for it is love that gives life its value. He will, therefore, cling to that Life with its Love, what- **XXVI.** ever sorrow may now overhang it, "whatever fickle tongues may say." Better that he should die, than that love should perish and become indifference. Better deep feeling and passion,

with all the pain that may come of them, than
the calm of a sluggish, indifferent
XXVII. heart.

> " I hold it true, whate'er befall ;
> I feel it, when I sorrow most ;
> 'T is better to have loved and lost
> Than never to have loved at all." [1]

[1] Compare Goethe's lines, *Faust*, Pt. II. vv. 1659–60:

> " Doch im Erstarren such' ich nicht mein Heil,
> Das Schaudern ist der Menschheit bestes Theil."

and vv. 2847–8 :

> " Geheilt will ich nicht sein ! mein Sinn ist mächtig !
> Da wär ich ja wie andre niederträchtig."

CHAPTER IV.

(xxviii–xxxvii.)

Turning from the past to the future. The immortality of the soul. The hope coming from revelation confirmed by reason. Reason and Revelation.

AT this point the poet begins to take some interest in the affairs of life, and to turn from the past to the future. Christmas has come, with its merry bells proclaiming " peace and goodwill to all mankind " and bringing him " sorrow touched with joy,"[1] joy engendered by hope. In spite of the grief that lies over the house, and in which even XXVIII. the skies seem to participate, the old Christmas formalities and pastimes are kept up. But the gladness which such XXIX. things are meant to attest comes not, only

> " an awful sense
> Of one mute Shadow, watching all."

Under the influence of this felt presence of the loved and lost, the be- XXX.

---

[1] Compare with this the effect of the Easter bells upon Faust, in bringing him back to hope and preventing suicide. Goethe's *Faust*, Pt. I.

reaved take each other's hands and, with tear-
bedimmed eyes and echo-like voices, sing im-
petuously a merry song they sang with him
shortly before his death.   But the invisible
presence and the Christmas season bring a
more solemn and a more hopeful feeling, under the inspiration of which they sing with assurance of the immortality of the soul, the
"keen seraphic flame," and encourage each
other to hope.

> "They do not die
> Nor lose their mortal sympathy,
> Nor change to us, although they change.

> "Rapt from the fickle and the frail
>   With gather'd power, yet the same,
>   Pierces the keen seraphic flame
> From orb to orb, from veil to veil."

The hope offered by the Christian revelation
recalls the story of Lazarus, and the
XXXI. poet wonders why, if he was really
dead and restored to life, we are not told what
he had to relate of the life beyond the grave.
He concludes :

> "He told it not; or something seal'd
> The lips of that Evangelist."

His sister, Mary, would have all curiosity on
the subject quenched by joy, love, and
XXXII. reverence, feelings far higher than
"curious fears," which come only to the un-
happy.

"Thrice blest whose lives are faithful prayers,
    Whose loves in higher love endure;
    What souls possess themselves so pure,
Or is there blessedness like theirs?"

And this leads the poet to warn those who, after much battling with doubt and difficulty, have attained a purely rational faith, that   XXXIII.

      "has centre everywhere
    Nor cares to fix itself to form,"

not to disturb the faith-through-form of their sisters, of those simple souls, who are made happy and eager for good by their childhood's beliefs. A second conscience, in the form of an external ideal, is a valuable and often needful addition to "the law within," "in a world of sin."

But, after all, it ought not to require any revealed, supernatural proof to convince us of the soul's immortality.   XXXIV. The very dimness and imperfection of our lives here, compared with the perfection we imagine and aspire to, ought to suffice. If those ideals and aspirations which give life its meaning are but delusions, then all is vain, the universe a mockery, justice a cruel chimera, and God a lie. Then

    "'T were best at once to sink to peace,
      Like birds the charming serpent draws,
      To drop head-foremost in the jaws
    Of vacant darkness and to cease."

Notwithstanding this verdict of the reason,
the poet is willing to consider the
case so often put by those who cannot see their way to belief in immortality:
Supposing by some inconceivable means we
could be convinced that death ends all, would
it not still be worth while, for the sake of
the sweetness of love, to cling to this life? Is
not human life worth living for its own sake?
He replies in the negative, for the reason that
the very sweetness and worth of love are due
to the feeling that it is divine and eternal.
Take away this feeling, convince men that the
world is governed by brute force, not by love,
and love will lose its sweetness, and die from
fear of death.   The case is an idle one.

> "If Death were seen
> At first as Death, Love had not been,
> Or been in narrowest working shut,
>
> "Mere fellowship of sluggish moods,
> Or in its coarsest Satyr-shape
> Had bruised the herb and crush'd the grape
> And bask'd and batten'd in the woods."

In a word, love unglorified by the feeling of
immortality would sink down into mere brute
passion.   Hence, unless life be immortal, it
contains nothing to make it worth living.

Many persons at the present day will, no
doubt, question the justice of this conclusion,
and agree with Goethe that "existence is a

duty, were it but for a moment." Indeed, it
seems to be the tendency of thought at the
present moment to find a satisfactory formula,
that is, a moral and religious motive, for this
life, without any reference whatever to a life
beyond. That life without such reference
could and would be, nay, has been, lived, is
certain; but whether it could long so main-
tain itself on moral heights, whether, indeed,
there is any satisfactory moral formula for
such a life, seems to me very questionable.
One thing is certain: no such formula has
been found, and the evident failure of the
numerous quests recently made points to the
conclusion that probably none can be found.

Although our human reason, when subtly
questioned, is sufficient to reveal to us God,
Freedom, and Immortality,

> " Tho' truths in manhood darkly join,
>   Deep-seated in our mystic frame,"

this fact does not remove the necessity for another revelation, suited to those minds which
are incapable of such subtle questioning. Hence the value of the Christian XXXVI.
mythus, that "truth embodied in a tale." It
can "enter in at lowly doors," which would be
barred against "truth in closest words."

But, in speaking thus of Christianity, as a
sort of " Picture-Writing to assist the weaker

faculty,"[1] the poet feels that he has broached a delicate subject. The heavenly Muse of revelation (Urania) reproves him sharply, and

XXXVII.
tells him to confine himself to his own pagan sphere. His pagan Muse (Melpomene) replies meekly, confesses her unworthiness, and pleads for indulgence on account of her need for comfort.

> " I murmur'd as I came along,
>   Of comfort clasp'd in truth reveal'd,
>   And loiter'd in the master's field,
> And darken'd sanctities with song."

[1] Carlyle, *Sartor Resartus*, Bk. II. chap. ix.

CHAPTER V.

(xxxviii–xlviii.)

The simple conviction of immortality does not satisfy the heart, which desires to realize immortal life and communicate with the departed. Metempsychosis.

THOUGH convinced by reason, confirmed by revelation, that life is immortal, and that his friend still exists, the poet yet finds his heart unsatisfied. The want of power to realize his friend's condition, or to establish any form of communication with him, leaves therein a weary, aching, dark, paralyzing void, lighted only by the doubtful gleam coming from the songs which he loves to sing, and which, he hopes, by pleasing the departed, may hold his attention. And so the for- XXXVIII. mer darkness, after being slightly dissipated, returns. The gloom of the old stone-grasping, skull-knitting yew, into which, through numbing sorrow, he had grown "incorporate," (ii.)

XXXIX.

"is kindled at the tips,
And passes into gloom again."

Such, at least, is the whisper of Sorrow.

But the poet is aware that she lies, and employs his fancy in trying to realize the condition of the spirit of his friend. He would fain think of it as a bride, that has left a loving

XL. father's house to go to a home full of new love and new hopes, and in some respects the comparison answers ; but alas ! the difference is too palpable. The bride will from time to time return to gladden the scenes of her maidenhood, " And bring her babe, and make her boast ; "

> " But thou and I have shaken hands,
>   Till growing winters lay me low ;
>   My paths are in the fields I know,
> And thine in undiscover'd lands."

Feeling the failure of this attempt, the poet

XLI. tries to conceive an act of will by which he should be able

> " To leap the grades of life and light
> And flash at once "

upon his friend. But this is folly. He cannot reach him, and at times there comes upon him a chilling, " spectral doubt " that he shall never reach him, but be " evermore a life behind," the difference in their grade of spiritual development holding them, like gravitation, in different spheres. But this he recog-

XLII. nizes to be a foolish fancy. Such difference does not confine souls to different spheres, else he and his friend, who

was so much his superior, could never have
walked upon the same earth. And so he may
hope to overtake his friend, and learn from him
the results of his spiritual experience.[1]

> " And what delights can equal those
>   That stir the spirit's inner deeps,
>   When one that loves but knows not, reaps
> A truth from one that loves and knows ? "

Thus far the poet has considered only the
Christian view of immortality, which holds that
the soul is created by God at the birth of the
body, is incarnated but once, and, after one
probation, passes to a condition unalterable
for all eternity. But other views of immortality have been held. Among the most common of these is metempsychosis, or the belief
that every soul is everlasting, and is, or may
be, incarnated an indefinite number of times.
Of this there are two chief forms, the Greek
and the Buddhistic. To these the poet now
turns.

If the soul is incarnated many times, then
death is but a longer and deeper
sleep, and life and death alternate   XLIII.
like waking and sleeping. During death, the

---

[1] Compare the opposite view, Goethe, *Faust*, Pt. II.
vv. 7467 *sqq.*

> " Wir wurden früh entfernt
>   Von Lebechören ;
>   Doch dieser hat gelernt,
>   Er wird uns lehren."

disembodied spirit, though unconscious, retains, in latent form, all the impressions and experience of all its past lives, and thus the entire experience of the world is treasured up, unimpaired, in "that still garden of the souls." In this case also the poet may expect in another life to know and love his friend, and to be known and loved by him.

But, if our present life is only one of many lives, past and to come, does not the fact that we have now no remembrance of any past life raise a presumption that those who pass into another life will have no remembrance of what happened in this, but will have to be-XLIV. gin existence there as children without experience ? But the poet doubts whether man has not even in this life some dim recollections of past lives :

"perhaps the hoarding sense
Gives out at times (he knows not whence)
A little flash, a mystic hint." [1]

So, in the higher life, there may come to his friend "some dim touch of earthly things," and the poet begs :

[1] Pythagoras, the founder of the Greek doctrine of metempsychosis, is said to have remembered all his past lives, to have recognized on the door of a temple the shield which, as Euphorbos, he wore in the Trojan war, and to have discovered the soul of an old friend in a dog that some one was whipping. There are some facts in our psychic life which certainly suggest the thought of lives previous to this.

" If such a dreamy touch should fall,
　　O turn thee round, resolve the doubt ;
　　My guardian angel will speak out
In that high place, and tell thee all."

But, after all, this may be our first conscious
life, for which the others were mere prepara-
tions. Indeed, the very purpose of XLV.
this embodiment of ours may be to
render us conscious of our own individuality,
our separateness from the great universe of
being, our identity, which is a matter of memory ; and this consciousness, once gained, may
be eternal. Incarnation would seem useless,
if, at the dissolution of the body, man lost his
individuality and identity, and had to acquire
them afresh in each new life. But, granting
that in the next life we shall retain the consciousness of our identity gained here, it does
not follow that we shall remember the events of
this life with any clearness, since we observe
that, in proportion as we grow older here, we
forget the events of our earlier life, its sorrows
and joys, " thorn and flower." Were
it not so, life would "fail in looking XLVI.
back ; " that is, it would take a life-time to recall the events of a life-time. But these facts
are all due to the form of time, or succession,
under which we think. In the higher life, in
which spirits will think under the form of
eternity (*sub specie æternitatis*), an all-embra-
cing present without past or future,

> "clear from marge to marge shall bloom
> The eternal landscape of the past."

In that landscape the years of friendship will seem the richest field, but may shed their radiance on the whole.

The Buddhistic notion, that at death the individual soul loses its identity, "remerging in the general Soul, is faith as vague as all unsweet." It satisfies neither head nor heart. It teaches that the Infinite and Absolute Being is utterly without form or determination, and all forms, or individuals, appearing in the universe are mere temporary illusions. This doctrine, which leads men to seek the annihilation of Self, as a deluding phantasm, has several times tried to insinuate itself into Western thought; for example, through the Arabs in the twelfth century, and at present, in the form of Monism, and as the outcome of physical science. Indeed, in all cases, the doctrine has its origin in thought carried on in terms of physics. Against it the Church, holding fast to the Aristotelian doctrine of the eternity of forms,[1] has always exerted herself to the utmost, and for a very good reason. Since, in mediæval terminology, the rational or intellective soul is the " substantial

XLVII.

---

[1] *Metaphys.*, vi. 8: 1033*b* 5 *sqq.*, 16 *sqq.* Cf. Thomas Aquinas, *Quæst. Quodlib.*, ix. art. 11.

form " of the body,[1] if forms are not eternal,
then the soul is not immortal. We might almost say that herein lies the fundamental distinction between the thought of the East and
that of the West. True to the latter, the poet
exclaims :

> " Eternal form shall still divide
> The eternal soul from all beside,
> And I shall know him when we meet."

In the spiritual world there will still be distinction of persons, still fellowship, still love ; and
however far isolation may be lost, as souls
enter into closer union, it will be lost in light,
not in darkness, in *nirvâṇa*.[2] As St. Bernard
puts it : "The substance (of the individual)
will remain, but in other form, other glory,

---

[1] This was laid down expressly, as a dogma of the
Church, in the Council of Vienne (1311), in this wise :
" Doctrinam omnem, seu positionem temere asserentem
aut vertentem in dubium quod substantia animæ rationalis aut intellectivæ vere ac per se humani corporis non
sit forma, velut erroneam, et veritati Catholicæ fidei in-
imicam, Sacro approbante Concilio, reprobamus : defi-
nientes ut si quisquam deinceps asserere, defendere, seu
tenere pertinaciter præsumpserit, quod Anima rationalis
seu intellectiva non est forma corporis humani per se et
essentialiter, tanquam hæreticus sit censendus." This
was even more strongly expressed by the Lateran Council (1515).

[2] *Nirvâṇa* means "the blowing out, the extinction of
light." See Max Müller, *Chips from a German Work-
shop*, i. 276.

other power. . . . So to be affected is to be deified." [1]

In closing this section of his poem, the author begs his readers not to look upon his "brief lays of Sorrow born," as if they contained definite solutions of the profound problems touched upon in them. Sorrow aspires to nothing so lofty :

XLVIII.

> " Her care is not to part and prove,
>   She takes, when harsher moods remit,
>   What slender shade of doubt may flit,
> And makes it vassal unto love."

[1] " Manebit quidem substantia, sed in alia forma, alia gloria, alia potentia. . . . Sic affici est deificari." *De diligendo Deo*, x. 28.

CHAPTER VI.

(xlix–lviii.)

More problems. The problem of Evil and Death. The conflict of Nature and Faith.

THE poet resolves to continue his treatment of all the doubts, hints, and fancies that rise, like ripples on the great, ever-deepening ocean of sorrow, and catch broken gleams from all directions, "From art, from nature, from the schools." Before undertaking this work, he offers a kind of prayer to the spirit of his friend, begging it to be near him at all times, when his spiritual powers are low or confused, to ward off depression, despair, and cynicism, and also in old age and death : XLIX.

L.

> " Be near me when I fade away,
>   To point the term of human strife,
>   And on the low dark verge of life
> The twilight of eternal day."

But here a doubt springs up : Do we really wish that the spirits of our friends should stand by us and look into our inmost thoughts? LI.

> " Is there no baseness we would hide ?
> No inner vileness that we dread ? "

But this doubt vanishes when he thinks of the majesty of death :

> "There must be wisdom with great Death,
> The dead shall look me thro' and thro'."

Still, although the dead see "with larger other eyes than ours," they must see defects in us. These exist, however high our inner or outer ideal may be. The poet complains that the living ideal which he had found in his friend does not suffice to draw him up to its height. But the same is true of all ideals, even the Christian one,

LII.

> "the sinless years
> That breathed beneath the Syrian blue."

A man must not fret, therefore,

> "That life is dash'd with flecks of sin,"

but try to offset the evil in him by a strong, steady endeavor after virtue, so that in the end,

> "When Time hath sunder'd shell from pearl,"

he may have a "wealth" of good to his credit.

This suggests the whole question of the function of evil in the world, a question which faith finds extremely baffling. How can we reconcile the existence of evil and pain with divine goodness ? Is evil ultimate, essential, and eternal, or is it only a passing phenomenon, necessary to emphasize the good and to develop free will ? Is there an eternal hell, or only a temporary purgatory? These are questions that try men's souls. The modern mind finds it hard to entertain the ordinary Christian belief that evil is eternal, and tends more and more to regard it as good in disguise. This was Goethe's view. Mephistopheles is made to say of himself, "I am a part of that power that always wills the evil, and always does the good."[1] Tennyson, observing that many a man overcomes the heats, passions, and follies of youth, becomes "a sober man among his boys," and "wears his manhood hale and green," is tempted LIII. to adopt Goethe's view. He asks: Must the field of life be sown with "wild oats," ere it be fit to produce useful grain? At best it could be true only for those men who are strong enough to outlive the "heats of youth," not for those who succumb to them. But, even were it true for the first, it would be unwise to

> "preach it as a truth
> To those that eddy round and round,"

that is, those who are still in the whirlpool of passion. We must not allow the difficulty which "divine Philosophy" finds in drawing a clear line between good and evil to mislead us into confounding them, or trifling with the distinction between them. All such confusion is pandering to "the Lords of Hell."

[1] *Faust*, Pt. I. vv. 983 *sq.*

But, while we call evil evil, we cannot, if we believe that "the great heart of the world is just," convince ourselves that it is eternal for any being, or that anything has been brought LIV. into life for an end other than itself, or for no end at all. In God's world there cannot be any refuse or waste. Good will come at last to everything, even to the singed moth and the cloven worm. But alas! looking at the facts of life as they present themselves to us, we find much that cries out against this conviction. We

> "can but *trust* that good shall fall
> At last — far off — at last, to all,
> And every winter change to spring."

Such conviction comes not from knowledge, but from faith, that immediate, ineluctable demand of the heart for justice, from something in us as natural and imperious as the infant's dread of darkness and cry for the light.[1]

Yea, we cannot doubt that this innate demand for justice, this self-approving LV. something which desires that "no life may fail beyond the grave," is the most godlike thing in us. It comes of infinite love and mercy, the dearest attributes of God. Can that which is likest to God in us be a lie? And shall we allow ourselves to be induced to believe this by certain phenomena of nature,

---

[1] Compare cxxiv. 5, Introduction pp. 8 *sqq.*

whose meaning we cannot comprehend? Shall
we distrust the deepest utterances of our own
souls, and lend an ear to the inarticulate de-
liverances of rocks, plants, and brute beasts?
If we watch the procedure of Nature, as revealed in the fossiliferous rocks and in her
living processes, we seem to learn that she
cares only for types, and is absolutely indifferent to individuals :

> " of fifty seeds
> She often brings but one to bear."

It is hard for the understanding to reconcile
such facts with the faith that every living thing
has its aim,

> " That not one life shall be destroy'd
> Or cast as rubbish to the void,
> When God hath made the pile complete."

Finding no hope but in faith, the poet falls
with his burden upon that mystic stair which
leads " through darkness up to God," stretches
" lame hands of faith." calls to what he feels to
be supreme, — justice and love, — and " faintly
trusts the larger hope " of universal good.

There are few finer conceptions in modern
literature than that expressed in the lines,

> " the great world's altar-stairs
> That slope thro' darkness up to God."

That the way to God is a steep stair, rising
through night to light, is a familiar conception

with all mystics, with Bernard, Bonaventura, Dante. Even M. Renan says: "The path of the universe is shrouded in darkness, but it goes toward God."[1] But grandly original is the thought that this stair is an "altar-stair," and that the great world itself is an altar, upon which everything that lives, if it will save its life, must offer itself in sacrifice to God. Every step upwards is a step away from self and towards God, from darkness to light. At first the rays from above are faint; but they brighten as we proceed, until at last we reach the great altar-fire, which consumes the very last remnants of self, the cause of all the darkness.

But even if, with the Comtists and the majority of evolutionists, we could bring
LVI.   ourselves to accept the doctrine that Nature cares nothing for individuals, but only for types or races, and to find a satisfaction for all our aspirations in altruistic devotion to the interests of "Humanity," we should soon find ourselves deprived of even that satisfaction by the voice of Nature. We have but to examine the fossiliferous rocks and the soil of the earth to find that "a thousand types are gone."[2]

[1] *Book of Job*, Introduction.

[2] See Darwin, *Origin of Species*, chap. x., *On Extinction*. It must be remembered that this work did not appear till 1859, long after *In Memoriam* was given to the world.

Nature seems to say, "I care for nothing, all shall go." Some catastrophe or some change in natural conditions may extinguish the whole human race at any moment. Can we sacrifice ourselves for a humanity of which this may be the end? Reason revolts.

Nature says one thing, Reason, the voice of God, another. Nature says all living things are born to die, "the spirit doth but mean the breath":[1] Reason, looking at man and his life, his loves, his aspirations, his faith, his sufferings, his self-sacrifices, utterly rebels against this suggestion. If man's end is to be petrified into rocks, or blown about as dust, then he is a mockery of mockeries, and his life as futile as frail:

> "No more? A monster then, a dream,
>   A discord. Dragons of the prime
>   That tare each other in their slime,
> Were mellow music match'd with him."

And the poet, in his despair, longs for the voice of his departed friend, "to soothe and bless;" but feels that no complete solution of his difficulties can come, till we have passed "behind the veil" of flesh that hides from us the eternal realities.

It need hardly be said at the present day

[1] The Latin *spiritus*, the Greek πνεῦμα, ψυχή, and many other words used to designate the psychic principle, meant originally *breath*. All metaphysical terms are metaphors, borrowed from physics.

that, upon the question of the soul's immortality, Nature and natural science have nothing to say. Science deals solely with becoming (*Werden*), with phenomena and their order of succession; and the soul is not a phenomenon. It belongs to the intelligible world of unchanging realities, to which also belongs the faculty of faith, "the test of things not seen." Thus "God and Nature," Reason and Understanding, are not "at strife;" they only speak two different languages, and treat of two different worlds.

The poet's despairing mood does not last.

LVII. He feels it to be a wrong to the memory of his friend, and, rather than cherish it, he will accept his loss, and cease wasting and darkening the present by living solely in the past. But, in thus loosening his embrace upon the past, he feels that he is leaving half his life behind, and that without it he will pass away, and his activity come to a close. All that comforts him and binds him to life is the thought that his friend is "richly shrined" in his verse.[1] If objective immortality be impossible, he has secured for his friend at

---

[1] Compare Shakespeare, Sonnet XVIII.

> " But thy eternal summer shall not fade,
> Nor lose possession of that fair thou owest,
> Nor shall Death brag thou wander'st in his shade,
> When in eternal lines to time thou grow'st ;
> So long as men can breathe, or eyes can see,
> So long lives this, and this gives life to thee."

least a "subjective immortality," as the Comtists say.[1]   In the ears of all men "till hearing
dies," the poet's verses will sound like the
agonia, announcing

> "The passing of the sweetest soul
> That ever look'd with human eyes,"

or the requiem sung at a saint's enshrinement.

With such sepulchral accents of hopeless
resignation he tries to take leave of
the past and turn to the present;   LVIII.
but ere he can do so, the "high Muse," Faith,
bids him not darken human life with such
dolorous, fruitless dirges, adding

> "Abide a little longer here,
> And thou shalt take a nobler leave."

That is, cling to the past with all its joys and
sorrows a little longer, and thou shalt then be
able to yield it up and accept the present in a
mood nobler than that of mere blind resignation.   That past contains the "promise and
potency" of the future.   Cling to the Beatrice
of early faith, until she rise "from flesh to
spirit," until thou be able to behold her as
spirit ; then thou wilt gladly take leave of the
love that was manifested in the flesh, to glow
with a deeper love manifested in the spirit.
And this will be a nobler leave-taking.[2]

---

[1] See George Eliot, "O may I join the choir invisible," and parts of Swinburne's "Super Flumina Babylo-
nis."

[2] Cf. Dante, *Purg.*, xxx., xxxi.

CHAPTER VII.

(lix–lxxi.)

Acceptance of Sorrow, as a chastener. Hope. Play of the fancy. Visions of sleep and waking.

ACCORDINGLY, the poet accepts his Sorrow, takes it to his bosom as a wife, realizing that, in its milder moods at
LIX.
least, it may make him "wise and good," and, living side by side with Hope, cease to seem Sorrow at all. In this mood he is able to turn with composure to the past, and tries in imagination to conceive his present relation to his
LX.
friend. He feels like a simple village girl who has fallen in love with a man of higher rank than her own, and suffers from
LXI.
the consciousness of her inferiority. How poor must his mental and spiritual condition seem to one who, in heaven, has joined

" the circle of the wise,
The perfect flower of human time " ! [1]

[1] Here the poet had probably in his mind Dante's Rose of the Blessed. See *Paradiso*, cantos xxx., xxxii. Compare xxiii. 19 *sqq.*

Still, no one, not even the soul of Shakespeare of the sonnets, could have loved a friend more. Perhaps this may be a claim to attention; if not, if that love is too slight and un- LXII. worthy, then he is willing that his friend should look upon it as a boyish caprice, an idle tale, and turn away from it, with "a flying smile," to nobler loves. But he comforts himself with the thought that wide differences of condition do not always preclude sympathy. He himself has a certain pity and LXIII. affection even for horses and dogs: may not his friend, though as far exalted above him as he above these animals, have a certain compassionate feeling for him?

Another thought strikes him. His LXIV. friend may look back upon his earthly life and him, as a man who, having risen by his own efforts from a low condition to one of influence and command, looks back with pleasure and a certain longing to the village where he was born and the friends of his boyhood, still toiling away at their simple, rustic occupations.

But these are fancies, whose only aim is to work up a happy thought. His LXV. friend may assume any attitude toward him he pleases, so long as the bond between them is not broken. He is only anxious to believe that, just as something of his friend

lives and works in him, so something of him
LXVI. may live and work in his friend. And
now he begins to recognize that a certain humanizing effect has come from his loss.
The very desolation caused by it, like the
blank occasioned by loss of sight, has made
him easily pleased with trifles, but at the same
time "kindly with his kind." The removal
of some object of affection which is above us
often turns our affection to that which is be-
side or below us.

If, during the day, the poet's imagination is
LXVII. occupied with the glorified spirit of
his friend, at night it wanders to the
resting place of his body, seeing his memorial
tablet illumined by the moon, or glimmering
LXVIII. like a ghost in the gray dawn. Even
in sleep his fancy labors with images
of his friend. At one time, the years of friendship come up again in all their freshness; but
alas! when he turns to his friend, he finds a
darkening trouble in his eye. Sleep has transferred the distress in his own soul to the face
of his friend. A fine piece of psychological
LXIX. observation! At another time he
dreams of universal desolation. He
himself, crowned with thorns, is made the butt
of public scorn, until an angel with low voice
and bright look comes to his aid.

" He reach'd the glory of a hand,
    That seem'd to touch it into leaf:
    The voice was not the voice of grief,
    The words were hard to understand."

With the single exception of Dante, no poet
has made so many fine observations on the
visions of sleep as Tennyson. Perhaps even
finer are his observations on those waking visions which he and, apparently, all persons of
powerful imagination see, when they
gaze fixedly into the dark. These   LXX.
visions are entirely beyond the control of the
will. Accordingly, when the poet strives to
paint the features of his friend upon the
gloom among his waking visions, he finds he
cannot:
                    " the hues are faint
    And mix with hollow masks of night."

These masks go on tumbling and mixing at
their own pleasure, a strange, weird phantas-
magoria,

    " Till all at once *beyond the will*
        I hear a wizard music roll,
        And thro' a lattice on the soul
    Looks thy fair face and makes it still."

How often does the image which one has
vainly tried to conjure up flash of itself before the eye, when the will is quiescent!

Among the consistent dream-visions from
the past that come to the poet, the
most remarkable are those from a   LXXI.

summer tour which he made through France
with his friend in 1832.[1] So clear are these
visions that he begs " Sleep, kinsman to death
and trance and madness," to "bring an opiate
trebly strong," and not only call up the past
in all its reality and joy, but to blot out the
sense of loss and wrong that comes from the
present. So, in *sleep* at least, his friend will
be restored to him, in a way foreshadowing the
restoration that may be expected from Death.
Death may give completely what sleep can
give only blurred. So hope comes from many
quarters.

[1] Compare the poem, *In the Valley of Cauteretz.*

CHAPTER VIII.

(lxxii–lxxvii.)

*What his friend might have been. Vanity of
fame and of monuments.*

BUT the return of the anniversary of his
friend's death (September 15th) brings back
all the old feeling of loss, and sets
the poet's imagination to work, fancy-
ing all that might have been, had his friend
been spared. But he is not now in a rebellious
mood. True, the fame which he fore-
saw for his friend, as the reward of
much usefulness, has not been realized ; but
can he tell whether the world needed his
friend at all? "Great Nature is more wise
than I,"[1] he says elsewhere, and he says the
same here, in other words :

> " I curse not nature, no, nor death ;
> For nothing is that errs from law."

And, after all, what is fame? A mere shadow
that, even at the best, lasts for a few years,
but lays no hold on eternity. One can well
afford to dispense with the short-lived, sub-

LXXII.

LXXIII.

[1] *To J. S.*, v. 9.

jective immortality of the Comtists,[1] mere
fame to which its object is utterly insensible,
provided he obtain objective immortality, an
ever-widening and deepening conscious life.
What is even Shakespeare's fame compared
with eternal bliss? Dante, who was himself
by no means free from the "last infirmity of
noble mind," has expressed this with great
force and truth, in words placed in the mouth
of an enlightened soul in Purgatory:

"The rumor of the world is but a breath
Of wind, that now comes hence and now comes thence,
And changes name, because it changes sides.
    "What fame wilt thou have more, if old thou shed
From thee the flesh, than if thou hadst been dead
Ere thou hadst ceased to babble 'pap' and 'mon,'[2]
    "From hence a thousand years, which is a space
More brief to the eternal than a wink
Is to the circle that in heaven moves slowest?

.   .   .   .

    "Your fame is as the greenness of the grass,
That comes and goes, and he discolors it
Who made it issue tender from the earth."[3]

Indifference to fame naturally follows from
a firm belief in immortality. It is, therefore,

[1] See Comte's *Catéchisme Positiviste*, pp. 161 *sqq.*,
where this immortality is described in a very amusing,
not to say absurd, way.
[2] "Il *pappo* e il *dindi*," childish words for bread and
money.
[3] *Purg.*, xi. 100–8; 115–7.

peculiarly characteristic of sincere Christians.
Among pagans, fame was reckoned as one of
the noblest motives, as we see in the Homeric
poems and the *Edda.* In the latter we find
an excellent expression of the pagan feeling
on the subject: "Cattle die; friends die; a
man himself dies; but fame dies never to him
that gets it well."[1]

Thinking of the wise and great that have
earned fame worthily, the poet recognizes in his dead friend a family like- LXXIV.
ness to them, which he thinks might be worked
up into something compelling a recognition not unlike fame. But this LXXV.
elaboration he will not attempt, leaving his
friend's worth to be judged by the measure of
his own grief for his loss. Besides,

> "The world which credits what is done
> Is cold to all that might have been."

But his friend has found his sphere of work
elsewhere, and there, doubtless, his appointed
task

> "Is wrought with tumult of acclaim."

And even if he should choose to do for his
friend what Dante did for Beatrice,
raising to his interrupted career a LXXVI.
monument of glorifying verse, what would it

---

[1] *Hávamál.* 75; cf. 76.

profit? It too would perish in a few years,
"before the mouldering of a yew," "ere half
the lifetime of an oak." And, though
LXXVII. the poems of Homer still last, there
is no hope whatever for modern rhyme. It is
doomed to early oblivion :

> " But what of that ?   My darken'd ways
>   Shall ring with music all the same ;
>   To breathe my loss is more than fame,
> To utter love more sweet than praise."

CHAPTER IX.

(lxxviii–lxxxiii.)

Sorrow woven into life. The example of the friend followed. The moral world reconstructed.

ANOTHER Christmas comes, in whose festivities there is no sign of mourning for the departed,

LXXVIII.

> " No single tear, no mark of pain."

This does not mean that Sorrow is dead, or has ceased to exert her purifying influence :

> " No — mixt with all this mystic frame,
> Her deep relations are the same,
> But with long use her tears are dry."

She has been accepted and woven silently into life.

The family festivities suggest the thought that the poet might have been expected to find an object for his deepest affections among his own kin, whereas he has said (ix. 5.) that his friend was more to him than his brothers. He assures his brother [1]

LXXIX.

---

[1] Charles Tennyson, who afterwards changed his surname to Turner, was himself no mean poet. In 1827

that this implies no want of respect for him, who is worthy " to hold the costliest love in fee." But brothers are " one in kind," being moulded under the same influences, whereas the stranger often possesses a difference which gives zest to friendship.

> " And so my wealth resembles thine,
>   But he was rich where I was poor,
>   And he supplied my want the more
> As his unlikeness fitted mine."

LXXX.

The difference between himself and his friend suggests the question how the latter would have acted, had the case been reversed ; that is, had Tennyson died and Hallam been spared. He feels sure that the bereaved one would then have felt

> " A grief as deep as life or thought,
>   But stay'd in peace with God and man,"

turning his " burthen into gain." This example love prompts the poet to follow.

LXXXI.

Amid such thoughts as these, Sorrow is becoming so gracious that he is almost giving up his grudge against Death,

the two brothers published conjointly a small volume of poems, entitled " Poems by two Brothers," the contents of which appear in some American editions of Tennyson's poems. The second volume of *Macmillan's Magazine* (1860) contains four sonnets (pp. 98 *sq.*) and a versified legend (p. 226) by Charles Tennyson, who was a clergyman. The third brother, Frederick Tennyson, was also a poet.

when the thought strikes him that, had his
friend lived, he himself might have come to
know a yet deeper love than that of his youth,
and his grudge is renewed.

> " But Death returns an answer sweet :
>   ' My sudden frost was sudden gain,
>   And gave all ripeness to the grain
> It might have drawn from after-heat.' "

And so he again becomes reconciled to
Death's work, with only a little re-
sentment, because he cannot com- LXXXII.
municate with his friend. Altogether, a new
life is stirring in him, so full of receptivity and
energy that he is impatient with the
Spring because it comes too slowly LXXXIII. .
to be in sympathy with him and his feelings :

> " O thou, new-year, delaying long,
>   Delayest the sorrow in my blood,
>   That longs to burst a frozen bud,
> And flood a fresher throat with song."

In a word, the poet's shattered moral world
has been reconstructed, if not completely, at
least far enough to make rational, aimful activity possible for him. He has done with
what he calls " Confusions of a wasted
youth."

And here we may ask : What influences
have effected this reconstruction ? The answer is, Time and Reason. The former, by
dulling the emotional pain which converts the

visible world into chaos, has made it possible
for the understanding to recognize that " Nothing is that errs from law ": the second, intro-
ducing order into the moral chaos, which the
understanding always produces, finds justice
and love in the essence of things :

> " I *know* transplanted human worth
> Will bloom to profit otherwhere." (lxxii. 3.)

The injustice which the understanding finds
in temporal life Reason wipes out, by pointing
to eternal life. Justice is in the spiritual world
what mechanical law is in the material. These
two worlds constitute the moral world, wherein
man is called to choose and act.

CHAPTER X.

(lxxxiv–lxxxix.)

The " low beginnings of content," resulting in (1) *acceptance of loss,* (2) *new attachments,* (3) *power to dwell with pleasure in the past.*

In his altered mood, the poet is able to do three things impossible before : *First,* to contemplate, with only a slight reawakening of bitterness, the life that would have been his, if his friend had been spared ; *second,* to enter upon new friendships ; *third,* to live over again the past and revisit the scenes of it, with a certain delight.

(I.) The picture of the life that might have been is drawn with infinite tenderness and warmth. The poet sees his LXXXIV. friend daily growing in all the graces of manhood, "a central warmth diffusing bliss" on all his kin. which would have included himself.[1]

---

[1] Arthur Hallam was to have married Tennyson's sister Emily. Among his published *Remains* there are two poems referring to her, " To two Sisters," " To the loved One." Both are marked by exquisite purity and tenderness, such as we rarely find save in the Italian poets.

He sees him a power for good in society and
state, earning an honest, unsought fame among
men, and the approval of God.   He sees himself "an honor'd guest," walking by the side
of his friend through all the phases of a noble
life, rich in good, until at last

> " He that died in Holy Land
> Would reach us out the shining hand,
> And take us as a single soul."

Perhaps there does not exist in literature any
other description of a noble life equal to this,
unless it be that which occurs in the fourth
book (third ode) of Dante's *Convivio.*   The
following is a literal rendering :

> " The soul which this goodness adorns
> Holds it not within itself concealed ;
> For from the beginning, when it weds the body,
> It shows it even unto death.
> Obedient, sweet, and modest
> It is in its Earliest Age ;
> And it adorns its person with beauty
> Through the harmony of its parts.
> In Manhood temperate and strong,
> Full of love and courteous praise,
> And only in deeds of loyalty it takes delight.
> It is in its Old Age
> Prudent and just ; and generosity is heard of it ;
> And in itself it rejoices
> To hear and speak of others' good.
> Then in the Fourth Part of life
> It reweds itself to God,
> Contemplating the end which awaits it,
> And blesses the times that are past."

(II.) With the old conviction (xxvii. 4) confirmed that

> " 'T is better to have loved and lost
> Than never to have loved at all,"

the poet turns warmly to a second friend [1] of early days, who, with a view to alleviate their "common grief," has asked LXXXV. him, kindly but half reproachfully, about his condition, and whether sorrow for his loss has weakened his faith and hope in higher things, and blasted his affections. In true Dantesque fashion, he replies to all the three questions in turn. *First*, he tells of the years of sorrow long-drawn-out that followed his great loss, and how, notwithstanding his pain, he has found, through the influence of his friend, "in grief a strength reserved" preventing him from swerving "to works of weakness." He has continually recognized that the possession of a will free to choose life or death imposes on man heavy responsibilities of action :

> " Yet none could better know than I,
> How much of act at human hands
> The sense of human will demands,
> By which we dare to live or die."

[1] Who the friend is, is not apparent ; possibly E. L. Lushington, or Rev. W. H. Brookfield, on whose death the poet wrote a sonnet, containing these lines :

> " How oft with him we paced that walk of limes,
> Him, the lost light of those dawn-golden times,
> Who loved you well ! Now both are gone to rest."

Second, he gives assurance that grief has not undermined his faith, by telling what he believes with regard to his lost friend :

"God's finger touch'd him, and he slept.

"The great Intelligences fair [1]
  That range above our mortal state,
  In circle round the blessed gate,
Received and gave him welcome there ;

"And led him thro' the blissful climes,
  And show'd him in the fountain fresh
  All knowledge that the sons of flesh
Shall gather in the cycled times."

[1] "The movers of that [third heaven] are substances separate from matter, that is *Intelligences,* whom the common sort call *Angels.*" — Dante, *Convivio,* ii. 5. — "The First Agent, that is, God, impresses his power upon some things after the manner of a direct ray, and on others after the manner of a reflected splendor. Whence, on the *Intelligences* the divine Light radiates without medium; on the others it is reflected from these Intelligences that are first illuminated."—*Ibid.,* iii. 14. — "In certain books translated from the Arabic, separate substances, which we call *Angels,* are called *Intelligences,* perhaps for the reason that substances of this kind always have actual [never mere potential] intelligence. In books translated from the Greek, however, they are called *Intellects* or *Minds.*" — Thomas Aquinas, *Sum. Theol.,* Pt. I. q. 79, art. 10. Among the Christian Gnostics these intelligences were called *Æons* (αἰῶνες). These are mentioned even in the Epistle to the Hebrews, i. 2 : "By whom also He made the Æons" (αἰῶνας, curiously mistranslated 'worlds' and 'ages,' in our English versions).

Third, he affirms that his affections, so far from being blasted by grief, have been deepened and purified by it. He loves his lost friend with a friendship

> " Which masters Time indeed, and is
> Eternal, separate from fears :
> The all-assuming months and years
> Can take no part away from this."

Nay more, though every season, every wind and wave recall the " old affection of the tomb," that very affection seems to say to him :

> " Arise, and get thee forth and seek
> A friendship for the years to come."

Accordingly he accepts with pleasure the proffered affection of the other friend, and returns it, though still forced to admit,

> " I could not, if I would, transfer
> The whole I felt for him to you."

In a word, while loving the incomparable friend more than ever, yea, with the great passion of his life, his heart is still fresh and open to other affections.

He is now again in full sympathy with Nature, the sure sign of spiritual health ; the shadows of Doubt and Death are LXXXVI. lifted from his fancy, which now exultingly flies

> " From belt to belt of crimson seas
> On leagues of odor streaming far,

> To where in yonder orient star
> A hundred spirits whisper 'Peace.'"

(III.) The poet now revisits with delight Cambridge, where he and his friend had passed so many happy, fruitful days.[1] He gives us a charming picture of the best side of university life, and of Arthur Hallam, telling how in his rapt moments his fellows saw

LXXXVII.

> "The God within him light his face,

> " And seem to lift the form, and glow
> In azure orbits heavenly-wise ;
> And over those ethereal eyes
> The bar of Michael Angelo."[2]

The joy at the thought of all this, alternating with the sense of loss, makes the poet feel the fierce extremes of emotion ; so that, though he would " prelude woe," which is disharmony, he is mastered by the fundamental harmony of the universe :

LXXXVIII.

> "The glory of the sum of things
> Will flash along the chords and go."

We now get a picture of Hallam's visits to Tennyson's early home in Lincoln-shire, and of the family life at Som-

LXXXIX.

---

[1] Tennyson went to Cambridge in 1828 and there met Hallam.

[2] The portrait of Hallam prefixed to his *Remains* shows this bar, though but slightly. It is very marked in the portraits in profile of Michael Angelo.

ersby Rectory. And what an atmosphere of
simple happiness, love, and refinement! No
wonder that Hallam hated cities, which

> " merge . . . in form and gloss
> The picturesque of man and man."

CHAPTER XI.

(xc–xcvi.)

Desire still to see the friend in any form. Dif-
ficulties. Trance. Ecstatic union with the
glorified spirit. Vision of truth. Doubt.

HAVING thus, with much pain and struggle,
pieced together a new life, of which chasten-
ing sorrow is an essential element, the poet
asks himself how it would be if his friend
should now return to him and annihilate this
sorrow. Would he not be disconcerted, like
the heir to a great estate by the restoration of
his father to life, or a happy wife by the resus-
citation of an old, accepted lover?
No! no! The man who could feel so

XC.

> "tasted love with half his mind,
> Nor ever drank the inviolate spring
> Where nighest heaven."

Gladly would he have his friend return to him.

> "Ah dear, but come thou back to me :
> Whatever change the years have wrought,
> I find not yet one lonely thought
> That cries against my wish for thee."

Yea, he would be glad to have his friend come

back to him in two forms, to suit different
seasons ; in the spring assuming the
form he wore on earth ; in the warm,
XCI.
bright summer, his glorified form, appearing
" like a finer light in light." [1] At the same
time he realizes that, if his friend should appear to him, he might think the vision a mere hallucination. Nay, even
XCII.
if it should recall some event from their past
lives, he might take this for a trick of memory,
while, if it uttered prophecies or warnings
which afterwards came true, they would seem

> " But spiritual presentiments
> And such refraction of events
> As often rises ere they rise." [2]

From all this the poet wisely concludes :
" I shall not *see* thee." His friend,
now a glorified Intelligence, " sepa-
XCIII.
rate from matter," will not reveal himself to

---

[1] Compare the beautiful lines in Dante, *Parad.*, viii.
16 *sq.*

> " E come in fiamma favilla si vede,
> E come in voce voce si discerne," etc.

[2] In a biographical sketch of Henry Fitzmaurice Hallam, who, like his brother, died young, — a sketch written by (Sir) Henry Sumner Maine and Franklin Lushington and prefixed to the brother's *Remains,* — we find
this curious passage : " He was conscious nearly to the
last, and met his early death (of which his presenti-
ments for several years had been frequent and very sin-
gular) with calmness and fortitude " (p. lvi.).

the senses, which are related only to matter.
But is there no other, no direct means of communication between souls?[1] May not the
free spirit itself come,

> " Where all the nerve of sense is numb;
> Spirit to Spirit, Ghost to Ghost "?

And the poet begs his friend, if such possibility there be, to descend from his " sightless
range with gods," that is, from the invisible,
divine world, and to hear

> " The wish too strong for words to name ;
> That in this blindness of the frame
> My Ghost may *feel* that thine is near."[2]

In other words, he begs his friend to reveal
himself as pure spirit to pure spirit, which
alone would be true spiritual communication.[3]

[1] Cf. *Aylmer's Field :*

> " Star to star vibrates light : may soul to soul
> Strike thro' a finer element of her own? "

[2] St. Bonaventura, in speaking of the ecstatic union
of the soul with God, says : " In this transition, if it is
to be perfect, all intellectual activities must be aban-
doned, and the whole apex of affection transferred and
transformed into God.   But this is a mystical and most
secret thing, which no one knows save him who receives
it, no one receives save him who deserves it."— *Itinerarium Mentis in Deum*, chap. vii.

[3] Compare Lord Houghton's *Strangers Yet :*

> " Will it ever more be thus —
> Spirits still impervious ?
> Shall we ever fairly stand

But the question arises: What must be the internal condition of the man who may hope to have such spiritual com-
XCIV.
munications from the "silent, earnest spirit-realm"? He must be "pure at heart and sound in head," "with divine affections bold," his spirit "at peace with all." Only such a man can "call the spirits from their golden day."

> "They haunt the silence of the breast,
>   Imaginations calm and fair,
>   The memory like a cloudless air,
> The conscience as a sea at rest :
>
> "But when the heart is full of din,
>   And doubt beside the portal waits,
>   They can but listen at the gates,
> And hear the household jar within." [1]

In the quiet of a summer night, when all nature is ruled by a spirit of har-
XCV.
mony, the poet finds such a season

> Soul to soul, as hand to hand?
> Are the bounds eternal set
> To maintain us strangers yet."
>   *Cornhill Magazine*, vol. i. p. 448.

[1] Compare Shelley's exquisite lines :

> " I am as a spirit who has dwelt
> Within his heart of hearts, and I have felt
> His feelings, and have thought his thoughts, and known
> The inmost converse of his soul, the tone
> Unheard but in the silence of the blood,
> When all the pulses in their multitude
> Image the trembling calm of summer seas."

of inner calm, and, in order the better to place
his own soul in relation with that of his friend,
he reads "the noble letters of the dead."   As
he proceeds, love and faith and vigor all grow
strong.

> " So word by word, and line by line,
>   The dead man touch'd me from the past,
>   And all at once it seem'd at last
> His living soul was flash'd on mine."

But this is not the soul in its mundane, unde-
veloped condition : it is the soul that has seen
the ultimate reality and truth, which it now
imparts directly to the soul of the poet :

> " And mine in his was wound and whirl'd
>   About empyreal heights of thought,
>   And came on that which is, and caught
> The deep pulsations of the world,

> " Æonian music measuring out
>   The steps of Time — the shocks of Chance —
>   The blows of Death.   At length my trance
> Was cancell'd, stricken thro' with doubt."

That these lines record an actual experience
there can be no doubt.   The poet tells us that
he was in a trance.   Lest this assertion should
be regarded as a mere poetic phrase, it may
be well to say that Tennyson from very
early life has been subject to trances.   In
proof of this, I am allowed to quote from a
letter written by him in 1874 to a gentleman
in this country, who had sent him an essay on

certain remarkable mental effects of anæsthetics. He says: "I have never had any revelations through anæsthetics; but a kind of 'waking trance' (this for lack of a better word) I have frequently had quite up from boyhood when I have been all alone. This has often come upon me through repeating my own name to myself silently, till all at once as it were out of the intensity of the consciousness of individuality the individuality itself seemed to dissolve and fade away into boundless being — and this not a confused state but the clearest of the clearest, the surest of the surest, utterly beyond words — where death was an almost laughable impossibility — the loss of personality (if so it were) seeming no extinction but the only true life.

"I am ashamed of my feeble description. Have I not said the state is utterly beyond words? But in a moment when I come back to my normal state of 'sanity' I am ready to fight for *mein liebes Ich*, and hold that it will last for æons of æons."

In his trance,[1] the poet "came on that which is" (τὸ ὄντως ὄν), the ultimate reality, and from that point of view was able to see

---

[1] *Trance* is a corruption of the Latin *transitus*, a word used in the Middle Age to translate the Greek ἔκστασις or ecstasy. Equivalent expressions were *excessus mentalis*, *excessus mentis*, *raptus mentis*, *ascensio*, *extasis*.

the world as a perfect harmony, in which even Chance and Death were necessary and concordant elements.[1] That such experiences, though rare, have fallen to the lot of deeply religious souls in all ages is a fact most amply attested. Several cases are mentioned in the Bible. Of these the most remarkable is that of Paul the Apostle, recorded in the twelfth chapter of the second Epistle to the Corinthians. St. Thomas Aquinas discusses the nature of this ecstasy at great length,[2] and says : "The soul of man is sometimes rapt, when it is elevated by the divine spirit to supernatural things, with abstraction from sensible things." Whenever in the Bible the phrases " I was in the spirit," " the spirit of the Lord came upon me," etc., occur, they always imply ecstasy. St. Bonaventura relates that St. Francis of Assisi once fell into a trance, in which he saw a six-winged seraph, nailed to a cross, and that he ever afterwards bore the stigmata of the crucifixion.[3] And the whole delightful work, *The Soul's Progress in God*, is nothing but a guide to such ecstasy. Dante

---

[1] An exactly similar experience is claimed for Pythagoras, " that being outside of the body he heard a melodious harmony" ('Εκεῖνος ἔφη ὡς ἔξω γενόμενος τοῦ σώματος ἀκήκοα ἐμμελοῦς ἁρμονίας. Schol. Ambros. to Odyssey I. 371).

[2] *Sum. Theol.*, II.[2] q. clxxv.

[3] *Itinerar. Mentis in Deum*, chapp. i., vii.

tells us with regard to himself : "After this
sonnet there appeared to me a wonderful vision, in which I saw things that made me con-
clude to say no more of this blessed one until
such time as I could more worthily treat of
her."[1] The result was the *Divine Comedy.*

But it is not only among Christians that
such experiences have occurred. Not to men-
tion the trances ascribed in late times to Pythagoras, or the references to visions of the
Divine in Plato[2] and Aristotle,[3] we find Porphyry, in his biography of his master, Plotinus, saying that this philosopher had frequent
trances, in which he saw "that God who has
neither shape nor form (ἰδέα), and is exalted
above all intellect and all that is intelligible,"
four such trances having been vouchsafed during his own acquaintance with him. Nay, he
even goes farther, and affirms that he himself
had one such experience, in his sixty-eighth
year. To attain such states was the end and
aim of all Neoplatonic philosophy, as well as
of much Christian Gnosticism.

It appears, then, that certain persons of
pure and deeply religious nature, when under
the influence of a strong spiritual love, and
when their souls are calm, collected, and free
from the irritation of the senses, rise to a finer

---

[1] *Vita Nuova*, last chapter. [2] See *Symposium*, p. 211.
[3] *Metaphysics*, xii. 7 : 1072*b* 24.

form of consciousness, in which they become clearly and directly aware of those universal, spiritual energies which control the world, and which, in their very nature, are beyond the reach of ordinary sense-perception. With regard to such experiences these three facts are well attested : (1) That they are infinitely sweeter and more satisfying to the soul than any other ; (2) that they impart to the mind a certainty of higher things which nothing else gives; (3) that they cannot be expressed in human concepts or in human speech, except through vague symbols and parables, which point rather to blessedness than to knowledge. Paul tells us that he " heard things unspeakable (or unspoken) which a man may not utter." Dante says :

" Within that heaven which of His light takes most
　　Was I, and things beheld which to rehearse
　　Who thence descends hath neither wit nor words;
　Because, when it approacheth its desire,
　　Our intellect goes deep'ning down so far
　　That after it the memory cannot go.
　But yet whatever of the blessed realm
　　I had the power to treasure in my mind
　　Shall be the matter of the present song." [1]

And when at last he " comes on that which is," and sees the primal fount of being, he can distinguish nothing : he is only supremely blest.[2]

---

[1] *Parad.*, i. 4 *sqq.*　　　　　[2] See p. 25, note.

In words almost identical in meaning with those quoted above, Tennyson says of his trance :

> " Vague words ! but ah. how hard to frame
>   In matter-moulded forms of speech,
>   Or ev'n for intellect to reach
> Thro' memory that which I became." [1]

That such trances are closely akin to the deepest poetic insight is shown by the utterances of many true poets. Wordsworth's lines will occur to every one. They are quoted here as the highest modern expression of ecstasy :

> " Such was the Boy — but for the growing Youth
>   What soul was his, when, from the naked top
>   Of some bold headland he beheld the sun
>   Rise up and bathe the world in light ! He looked —
> Ocean and earth, the solid frame of earth
> And ocean's liquid mass beneath him lay
> In gladness and deep joy. The clouds were touched,
> And in their silent faces did he read
> Unutterable love. Sound needed none,
> Nor any voice of joy ; his spirit drank
> The spectacle : sensation, soul, and form
> All melted into him ; they swallowed up
> His animal being ; in them did he live,
> And by them did he live ; they were his life.
> In such access of mind, in such high hour
> Of visitation from the living God,

[1] Compare Dante, *Parad.*, i. 70 *sqq.*

> " Transhumanize to signify by words
> None may : but let th' example serve for those
> For whom grace holds th' experience in reserve."

Thought was not; in enjoyment it expired.
No thanks he breathed, he proffered no request;
Rapt into still communion which transcends
The imperfect offices of prayer and praise,
IIis mind was a thanksgiving to the power
That made him; it was blessedness and love." [1]

Goethe doubtless puts his own deepest insight into the *Chorus Mysticus*, with which he closes *Faust*, his great life-work :

" All the transient
Is but a parable;
The unattainable
Here grows attainment;
The indescribable —
IIere it is done."

It is perhaps worth while observing that, in the Prologue to *Faust*, Goethe makes the world seem a perfect harmony to the archangels, who see the principle and whole of it.[2]   Only to the narrow intellect of Mephistopheles is everything disharmony.

It has seemed necessary to dwell at some length on this matter of ecstasy, because it is, in a sense, the kernel of the whole poem, which everywhere teaches us that knowing is not the highest faculty of the soul, but that above it is another, which alone can give us the truths necessary for rational life.   This is

---

[1] *Excursion*, Bk. I.

[2] " Und alle deine hohen Werke
Sind herrlich wie am ersten Tag."

the faculty of faith, whose form is justice, and
which, when at its highest, sees justice or harmony everywhere. It has been shown that an
ecstatic vision of the absolute harmony has
been claimed by some of the purest and noblest of human kind. The question remains :
What is the value of such visions? Seeing
that they leave behind them no clear knowledge, but only certain blessed feelings that
seek expression in symbols or myths, often
strange and fanciful, like St. Francis' six-
winged seraph, what confidence can the understanding place in such symbols? Can they be
fairly interpreted so as to be a guide and stay
to human life? Every soul, it seems, must answer this question for itself, no matter whether
it has had the experience itself, or only learnt
of it from others. Tennyson at first could not
place full confidence in his vision. It

" Was cancell'd, stricken thro' with doubt."

Morning found him a skeptic.

Shall this doubt be put away, as something
base? The simple, tender spirit of
the sister says reverently: " Doubt   XCVI.
is Devil-born." He knows not : he might even
be inclined to admit this, were it not for the
example of his friend, who always "fought his
doubts." He knows that in the highest region
of the soul it is not doubt, but impurity. that
mars and darkens.

" Perplext in faith, but pure in deeds,
    At last he beat his music out.
    There lives more faith in honest doubt,
    Believe me, than in half the creeds. "

So, following his friend's example, he will fight his doubts and gather strength, not blinding his judgment. In this way he will arrive at that power

"Which makes the darkness and the light,
And dwells not in the light alone."

CHAPTER XII.

(xcvii–ciii.)

The presence of the lost one, as a universal spirit, begins to be felt, though only at times. The old sore still easily opened. A happy, significant dream.

THAT union with the universal which the poet experienced in his trance, if it has not convinced his understanding, has not been without its effect upon his feelings. He now finds his love reflected from all the world.

> "My love has talk'd with rocks and trees;
> He finds on misty mountain-ground
> His own vast shadow glory-crown'd;
> He sees himself in all he sees."

Toward his friend, who now lives "in vastness and in mystery," he feels like a wife who has remained in the simple household ways of her maidenhood, while her husband has risen to heights of thought or science which she cannot comprehend.

> "She knows not what his greatness is;
> For this, for all, she loves him more."

But, for all this, the sense of loss still re-

XCVIII. mains, ready to be galled by every event that breaks in upon the quiet tenor of life. Some one is going on a continental tour, in which he will visit Vienna. This recalls the fact that the loved one died in that city, and makes the old horror of it rankle. The poet has never seen, will never see, Vienna, which, despite all the glowing descriptions of it he has heard, he is prepared to regard as haunted by an evil fate.

The anniversary of his friend's death, though ushered in with all the beauty of the autumn,

XCIX. brings to him only cause for mourning. Still, it is no longer lonely grief. To all those for whom the day brings similar grief he feels that

> " To-day they count as kindred souls ;
> They know me not, but mourn with me."

The poet's family has to bid farewell to its

C. old home in Lincolnshire, and the scenes amid which he has so often wandered with his friend. The presence of the dear one is everywhere :

> "I find no place that does not breathe
> Some gracious memory of my friend."

> " And, leaving these, to pass away,
> I think once more he seems to die."

The old home will pass into new hands,

which will have no pious care for the many
things interwoven with the poet's
most tender feelings — the garden,
the brook, the grove;

> "And year by year our memory fades
> From all the circle of the hills."

He is bound to his native spot, not only by
the associations of a happy boyhood,
but also by the memories of blessed
hours passed there in converse with his friend,
and he cannot tell which tie is the stronger.
For a time they fight in his soul, but at last,
when he turns

> "To leave the pleasant fields and farms;
> They mix in one another's arms
> To one pure image of regret."

CI.

CII.

But on the night before leaving the old
home the poet has a Dantesque vision of his friend, which leaves a feeling of contentment in his soul. He dreams
that he is dwelling in a "palace of art." In
the centre of this stands a statue, which,
though veiled, he recognizes to be his friend,
and before which maidens play and sing of all
that is "wise and good and graceful." Sud-
denly a dove flies in, bearing "a summons from
the sea." The maidens, learning that he must
go, "weep and wail," but accompany him to
a "little shallop" lying in the stream below.
The shallop glides down the stream, which

CIII.

ever widens between vaster-growing banks, and, as it does so, the maidens gather strength, grace, and majesty, while the poet feels in himself

> "the thews of Anakim,[1]
> The pulses of a Titan's heart,"

and power to sing the mightiest and deepest of songs. At last they reach the great Ocean, and see before them a great, splendid ship, with the lost one standing on the deck. The poet boards her, and falls in silence on the neck of his friend ; whereat the maidens wail, and upbraid him for deserting them, who had so long faithfully served him. He is so rapt that he pays no heed to them ; but his friend bids them come aboard. They do so,

> "And while the wind began to sweep
> A music out of sheet and shroud,
> We steer'd her toward a crimson cloud
> That landlike slept along the deep."

This dream was, doubtless, a real experience. Still, there is no mistaking its resemblance, in some points, to the *Palace of Art*, in others, to *Recollections of the Arabian Nights*, and, in others still, to the *Passing of Arthur*. No one has yet told us where our dreams come from, or whether they all come from the same source. Who shall tell us? Dante, whose experience in such matters was deep and broad, says :

---

[1] Deuteron. ix. 2.

" O Fancy that dost steal us so at times
   From outer things, that we are unaware
   Though thousand trumpets round about us blare !
What moveth thee, if sense afford thee naught ?
   'T is light that moves thee, which in heaven takes
      form,
   Self-moved, or else thro' will that guides it down." [1]

He elsewhere speaks of the hour at which

     " our mind, a pilgrim most
  From flesh, and least enthralled by thoughts,
In power of vision is well-nigh divine." [2]

At all events, the poet can console himself
with the thought that, at the end of his earthly
career, he will meet, face to face, the friend
who has so long stood a veiled statue in the
halls of his soul, before whom every muse or
power of his spirit has made music, and that,
into the glorious ship of that new, double life,
these powers will accompany him in all their
integrity.

[1] *Purg.*, xvii. 13 *sqq.*
[2] *Purg.*, ix. 16 *sqq.*

CHAPTER XIII.

(civ–cxiv.)

*Though our life at present is full of disappoint-
ment and sorrow, the poet will embrace it, and
let sorrow make him wise.   The wisdom buried
with his friend.   Knowledge and Wisdom.*

ANOTHER Christmas finds the poet in a new
CIV. home, in which he feels himself a
stranger.   Here too the Christmas
bells ring ; but, alas !

> "Like strangers' voices here they sound,
>   In lands where not a memory strays,
>   Nor landmark breathes of other days,
> But all is new unhallow'd ground."

Removal too "has broke the bond of dying
CV. use."   This year there shall be no
Christmas celebration, no old-fash-
ioned merriment :

> "For who would keep an ancient form
> Thro' which the spirit breathes no more ?"

He will hold the night "solemn to the past."
There shall be no dance or motion, save that
of the gleaming worlds which brighten in the

cloudless east, whose revolutions mark the lapse of the ages. To these he prays:

> " Run out your measured arcs and lead
> The closing cycle rich in good."

When the midnight bells strike up, the poet breaks forth into a song, exhorting them to ring out the old epoch, with all its sin, its strife, and its suffering, and ring in the better time. In this noble song we have a foretaste of that fierce arraignment of the life of the present day which characterizes some of the poet's later productions. Deeply religious by nature, like his friend Carlyle, he cannot reconcile himself to a life which, having no eye for the spiritual world, and no ear for the thunders of Sinai, takes a golden calf for its God, and political economy for its moral law. And yet that is the life which the great majority of mankind in our day lead. No wonder that he cries out,

CVI.

> " Ring out the darkness of the land;
> Ring in the Christ that is to be."

Before we can ever again heartily celebrate Christmas, we must have a new Christ. The old one is dead, leaving the festival but an empty form. Rather than be guilty of the hypocrisy of adhering to it, he will celebrate the birthday of his glorified friend, that living ideal, which fills his soul with aspiration after all good.

CVII.

"We keep the day.   With festal cheer,
With books and music, surely we
Will drink to him, whate'er he be,
And sing the songs he loved to hear."

So, at least, he can be sincere.

But in spite of the materialism and wretchedness of the present life, he will not flee from it, shutting himself out from his kind, like a hermit, or stiffening into stone with grief, like Niobe.   "Faith without works is dead"; vacant aspiration utterly profitless. However potent a man's yearning be, he can imagine nothing in the highest heaven but his "own phantom chanting hymns"; nothing in the deepest abyss of death but "the reflex of a human face."[1]   Instead of spending his days in selfish, contemptuous seclusion, he will accept human life as he finds it, with all its disappointments and sorrows.   These will, at least, teach him some of the wisdom which his friend held in store.

CVIII.

"'T is held that sorrow makes us wise,
Whatever wisdom sleep with thee."

[1] Omar Khayyám has expressed this thought very forcibly, though in a different spirit :

"I sent my Soul through the Invisible,
Some letter of the After-life to spell:
      And by and by my Soul return'd to me,
And answer'd 'I Myself am Heav'n and Hell':

"Heav'n but the Vision of fulfill'd Desire,
And Hell the Shadow of a Soul on fire,
      Cast on the Darkness, into which Ourselves,
So late emerg'd from, shall so soon expire."

But, alas! how much wisdom does so sleep! And he proceeds to describe, in words such as only love can dictate, his CIX. friend's intellect, eloquence, artistic insight, lofty aspiration, moral purity, profound but temperate love of freedom, and, last, his manly tenderness :

> " And manhood fused with female grace
> In such a sort, the child would twine
> A trustful hand, unask'd, in thine,
> And find his comfort in thy face."

All these aspects of wisdom the poet has seen and loved. Shall they remain without effect upon him, merely because the bearer of them has been removed from sight ? Surely not ; and he goes on to describe the power exerted by his friend's wisdom upon all classes CX. of men, old and young, weak and strong, loyal and proud, the fawning hypocrite, the stern, the flippant, the brazen fool, and lastly upon himself, in whom it woke deep, un-fathomable spiritual love

> " that will not tire,
> And, born of love, the vague desire
> That spurs an imitative will."

All this wisdom was simple and genuine, the outcome of a " high nature, amorous CXI. of the good," no mere hypocrisy or play-acting, such as the " churl [1] in spirit " may

---

[1] *Eorlas and ceorlas*, earls and churls, is the Anglo-Saxon for " gentle and simple."

practise for fashion's sake. It was no mere
veneer covering a coarse, coltish nature, but
"the native growth of noble mind," of a soul
looking out from an eye

> " Where God and Nature met in light ;

> " And thus he bore without abuse
>   The grand old name of gentleman,[1]
>   Defamed by every charlatan,
>   And soil'd with all ignoble use."

Having seen such a miracle of perfection,
such a "novel power," so unlike anything else he has ever known, he
finds it hard to rise to any enthusiasm for the
"glorious insufficiencies" of other persons.
His friend was like a cloud-compelling Jove,
ruling the tempests of thought, and by faith
making serene the heaven of the soul. What
might not have been expected in the
future from such a man? The thought
that Sorrow is the nurse of Wisdom does not
quite console the poet for the disappointed
hopes of the world.

CXII.

CXIII.

> " 'T is held that sorrow makes us wise ;
>   Yet how much wisdom sleeps with thee
>   Which not alone had guided me,
>   But served the seasons that may rise."

The "might-have-been" still looms up in glorious regret-bringing proportions before him.

---

[1] See note on p. 99.

He sees his friend a pillar of state, the hero
of his age, by his example and energy guiding
humanity through tempest and shock of rationalism and revolt to a loftier plane of life, with
nobler issues. Here the poet clearly realizes
the nature of the conflict in which the world
is now engaged. It is a conflict between two
powers of the soul, understanding and faith,
or knowledge and wisdom. Faith or wisdom
has to embody itself in an institution with
symbolic observances, ere it can appeal to the
mass of mankind. Such an institution, if it is
not carefully watched, and its symbolism pre-
vented from being taken for the thing sym-
bolized, is sure to arrogate to itself divine
authority and encroach upon the institutions
of the understanding. In a word, the Church
continually tends to encroach upon the State,
in virtue of a pretended divine authority, and
the State under this influence continually tends
to claim authority by the grace of God. It
was against these tendencies that Dante wrote
his *De Monarchia*, the first great political trea-
tise of the modern world, and directed the bit-
terest invectives of his *Divine Comedy*.[1] It is
these tendencies that in recent times have
brought about Rationalism, that revolt of the
understanding against the higher reason. In
rebelling against the degenerate institutions of

[1] See *Parad.*, xxviii.

reason, the understanding has rebelled against reason itself, and so men have lost hold of the spiritual and the divine, and sought to content themselves with the material and the animal. This is the origin of the current philosophies, falsely so called, of our time, Comtism, Spencerism, and the rest, and of all the anarchic ideas, social and political, which daily crop up everywhere. Against these rationalistic and materialistic philosophies and their implications, Tennyson, like Carlyle, has made a lifelong protest, proclaiming that Faith or Wisdom is not to be confounded with the temporary institutions which claim to embody it, but is to be embraced, hoarded, and tended, as man's supreme treasure, though all institutions should perish. It is the Christ that was and "the Christ that is to be," "the Saviour of life unto life."

No one, the poet admits, would think of disparaging Knowledge, of railing against her beauty, or of setting limits to her progress in any region where she is fitted to go. But, in her revolt against Faith, she is like a vain, wanton boy that has just escaped from his mother's apron-string. She rushes heedlessly on

CXIV.

> "And leaps into the future chance,
> Submitting all things to desire."

And so, to quote from Mrs. Browning's de-

scription of the French, the votaries of Knowledge

> "threaten conflagration to the world,
> And rush with most unscrupulous logic on
> Impossible practice."[1]

This must not be. Knowledge must learn her
place, learn that

> "She is the second, not the first."[2]

She cannot attain any of those truths that give
value and meaning to life; hence, unless life
is to lose its aim, she, who is the child of
the mind only, must consent to be guided by
Wisdom, the child of the whole soul. Higher
and truer than any clear conclusion which the
understanding can draw from the physical
facts of Nature is the dim, half-formulated
conclusion which the soul draws in response
to its total experience physical and spiritual.
And the poet, addressing his friend, prays:

> "I would the great world grew like thee,
>   Who grewest not alone in power
>   And knowledge, but by year and hour
> In reverence and in charity."

[1] *Aurora Leigh*, Bk. VI.
[2] Compare Prologue, vv. 5-8, and the poem, "Love
thou thy Land with Love far-brought." (v. 5.)

CHAPTER XIV.

(cxv–cxxiv.)

The return of spring reawakens hope, which soon ripens into faith and confidence.

AMID the new scenes into which the poet
CXV. has moved the spring returns, and
this time enters even into his breast
with its inspiring promise, making the deep
regret planted there blossom like an April
violet. But blossoming regret is not the only
flower in the spring-garden of the
CXVI. poet's heart. Faith and hope blossom too. The music, stir, and life of spring

> " Cry thro' the sense to hearten trust
> In that which made the world so fair."

Regret for the "days of happy commune dead"
is still there; but it grows weak in proportion
as faith waxes strong. The past, with all its
rare, lost delights, fades, as the more glorious,
spiritual future, with still rarer delights, looms
up in the soul. In this mood he is
CXVII. ready to be grateful for the temporary
separation from his friend, since it will only
serve to make reunion more blissful.

> " O days and hours, your work is this,
>   To hold me from my proper place,
>   A little while from his embrace,
> For fuller gain of after bliss."

Bliss is deepened by contrast with misery.

Nature, when he last consulted her, in his dark mood (lv., lvi.), suggested only thoughts of despair; now, in his brighter mood, he can draw from her suggestions of hope. Then he had only regarded the dead forms of Nature; now, he contemplates the whole of her living process, and finds that she is no feeble thing, but a " giant laboring in his youth." Human love and truth are part of that living process, and have no resemblance to the " earth and lime " of the fossil skeletons of extinct animals. The bearers of this love and truth, though they have left their dust behind them, and become to us invisible, we may trust,

CXVIII.

> " Are breathers of an ampler day
> For ever nobler ends."

The process of Nature is an endless development from lower to higher; and this process accomplishes itself, not only in the race as a whole, but in the individual, if he will only take it up and realize it in himself:

> " If so he type this work of time

> " Within himself, from more to more."

But this is no easy task, to be achieved by a

man who lies still like "idle ore." It demands one who is prepared to be as

> " iron dug from central gloom,
> And heated hot with burning fears,
> And dipt in baths of hissing tears,
> And batter'd with the shocks of doom

> " To shape and use."

Such a man will " move his course "

> " crown'd with attributes of woe
> Like glories."

And the poet calls upon men to

> " Arise and fly
> The reeling Faun, the sensual feast ;
> Move upward, working out the beast,
> And let the ape and tiger die."

Man's salvation depends upon his becoming a microcosm, and realizing the whole universe and all the process of it within himself; for only the universal is eternal.

> " Our wills are ours, we know not how;
> Our wills are ours, to make them thine."[1]

In this exalted frame of mind, he can now
CXIX.   return with delight to the old home of his friend.

[1] Prologue, v. 4.   Compare Swinburne's lines :

> " Unto each man his handiwork, unto each his crown
>   The just Fate gives;
> Whoso takes upon him the world's life, and his own lays down,
>   He, dying so, lives."
>   *Super Flumina Babylonis.*

> " Not as one who weeps
> I come once more."

He no longer finds " the long unlovely street "
(vii.) ; no longer

> " ghastly thro' the drizzling rain
> On the bald street breaks the blank day."

He can now " smell the meadow in the street,"
and feel all the charm of awakening nature ;

> " And in my thoughts with scarce a sigh
> I take the pressure of thine hand."

After much struggle with doubt born of
sorrow, the poet has at last come
back to entire conviction of the truth
of immortality. The law of justice revealed
in his own soul proclaims the annihilation of
that which has love and faith to be a moral
absurdity. The materialistic philosophy of
Locke and his followers, which rules our time
and claims to be confirmed by science, is a
cruel error based upon imperfect thinking.
The spiritual is not a mere function of the
material, a harmony of nerve-fibres. It is the
true reality, to which the material is but a
vision. As Thomas Aquinas so well puts it,
" The soul is not in the body as the contained,
but as the container." [1] If science could prove

cxx.

---

[1] *Sum. Theol.*, I. q. 52, art. 1. Compare Carlyle's in-
dignant protest : " Can the Earth, which is but dead
and a vision, resist Spirits, which have reality and are
alive ? " — *Sartor Resartus*, Bk. III. chap. viii.

that we are "wholly brain, magnetic mockeries," "cunning casts in clay," then what
would be the use of science to such transient
phantoms? Such a thing may be good for
apes; but no man with the aspirations of a
man would tolerate it. Death, which so fright-
CXXI.   ens the timid soul, is but as the even-
ing-star sinking below the horizon, to
rise again with renewed vigor and freshness,
as the morning-star, to usher in a new dawn.
Hesper and Phosphor are the same star in
different places. One is here reminded of
Sappho's beautiful line,

" Hesper, thou bringest all that the glimmering Dawn
    dispersed "; [1]

and of Plato's elegiacs, so exquisitely rendered
by Shelley :

" Thou wert the morning star among the living,
    Ere thy fair light had fled : —
Now, having died, thou art as Hesperus, giving
    New splendor to the dead." [2]

The poet can now revert with faith to his
CXXII.   trance (xcv.), which was "cancell'd,
stricken thro' with doubt." He can
believe that in that wonderful experience,
wherein he became conscious of the all-pervad-

---

[1] ϝέσπερε, πάντα φέρεις ὅσα φαίνολις ἐσκέδασ' Αὖως.

Frag. 95 (Bergk).

[2] Ἀστὴρ πρὶν μὲν ἔλαμπες ἐνὶ ζωοῖσιν Ἐῷος,
νῦν δὲ θανὼν λάμπεις Ἕσπερος ἐν φθιμένοις.

Epigr. 15 (Bergk).

ing law of the universe, his soul was really
wrapt round by that of his friend. If so, he
begs him to come to him now, invading heart
and head :

"And enter in at breast and brow,"

so that, in the enthusiasm of a vernal faith,
"as in the former flash of joy" (xcv. 9), he
may rise above the phenomenal world of life
and death, into the world of pure, eternal
ideas, the souls and sources of all glory and
all beauty. From that watch-tower of the
angels he can look calmly upon the
world of change, and defy its cruel CXXIII.
suggestions. He was wrong in questioning
Nature at all respecting the spirit's destiny.
To her spirit means but breath ;

"But in my spirit will I dwell,
     And dream my dream, and hold it true;
     For tho' my lips may breathe adieu,
     I cannot think the thing farewell."

At last he sees that the annihilation of a self-
conscious spirit is utterly unthinkable. But it
is not in nature or to the understanding that
this is revealed ; it is in spirit and to
faith. Nay, it is only there that God CXXIV.
Himself is to be discovered.

"I found Him not in world or sun,
     Or eagle's wing, or insect's eye ;
     Nor thro' the questions men may try,
     The petty cobwebs we have spun."

Nay, the understanding cannot even tell
whether God is to be thought as " He, They,
One," or " All," whether as " within " or " without." In other words, it cannot decide between Theism, Polytheism, Monotheism, and
Pantheism,[1] or tell us whether God is imma-
nent or transcendent. It is in the heart that
God is to be found. When the understanding
says there is no God, or that God is beyond
human apprehension, the heart rises up " like
a man in wrath," — " no, like a child in doubt
and fear," and answers : " ' I have felt,' " that
is, I have had experience, which no bugbears
of nature or subtleties of understanding can
ever make me disown or discredit. The very
rebellion of the heart against the head, of
reason against understanding, is the work of
the God within or present :

> " that blind clamor made me wise ;
> Then was I as a child that cries,
> But, crying, knows his father near ;

> " And what I am [2] beheld again
> What is, and no man understands ;

[1] Goethe, writing to Jacobi in 1813, says : " I, for
my part, with the manifold tendencies of my nature, do
not find one aspect of the divine enough. As a poet, I
am a polytheist ; as an investigator of nature, I am a
pantheist, and both in the same degree. If I require a
personal God *for my personality as a moral being, this
also is provided for in my mental constitution.*"

[2] The earlier editions read ' seem ' for ' am ' here.

And out of darkness came the hands
That reach thro' nature, moulding men."

The deep intuition which tells us that things are
as they are (for example, that the will is free)
is not to be shaken or undermined by the im-
potence of the understanding to comprehend
how or *why* they are as they are. Understanding in all cases makes an appeal to the
imagination, and within the jurisdiction of that
the things of the spirit do not come.

CHAPTER XV.

(cxxv–cxxxi.)

*Faith, Hope, and Love all intact. The greatest
is Love, without which Faith would be weak.*

HOPE being now restored, the poet recognizes that, in all his dark surmisings,
he has never really lost her :

CXXV.

> "She did but look thro' dimmer eyes ;
> Or Love but play'd with gracious lies,[1]
> Because he felt so fix'd in truth."

But whatever he may have said or sung was
inspired by the spirit of the matchless friend,
who, he now knows, will be with him until they
embrace again on "the mystic deeps," on the
deck of that great ship which steers across the
ocean of eternity (ciii.). In all that he
has done, or yet does, Love has been
his Lord and King,[2] and, under the guardian-

CXXVI.

---

[1] Compare Dante's definition of allegory — "a truth
hidden under a beautiful lie." (*Feast*, Tr. II. chap. i.)

[2] Dante speaking of his first meeting with Beatrice,
says : "From that time on I say that Love was Lord of
my soul, which was thus early wedded to him, and he
began to assume such assurance and such lordship over

ship of that king, he can sleep securely through the darkness of this flesh-blinded mortal life,

> "And hear at times a sentinel
>   Who moves about from place to place,
>   And whispers to the worlds of space,
> In the deep night, that all is well.

> "And all *is* well, tho' faith and form
>   Be sunder'd in the night of fear."

"We walk by faith, and not by form." The faith which belongs to the reason has, in these dark times of ours, been sun- CXXVII. dered from the form which belongs to the understanding. Our hearts are at war with our heads. Our hearts imperiously demand justice and ultimate good for all; our heads are puzzled when we see injustice triumphing and thousands of our fellow beings, who have fought for justice, perishing in what seems a hopeless struggle. But it is only to our contracted vision that it seems hopeless. If we would but open the ears of Faith, we should hear "a deeper voice across the storm" of convulsion, proclaiming the ultimate triumph

me, through the power which my imagination gave him, that I was obliged to do all his pleasure completely." *New Life*, chap. i. In many other places of this book Dante speaks of Love as his Lord. Compare *Purgatory*, xxiv. 52 *sqq.*

> "I am one who, when
> Love breathes, record, and in whatever mood
> He dictates in my heart, I signify."

of truth and justice, no matter if three more French Revolutions, each bloodier than another, should have to be passed through first. True, the times look threatening for that order of things which produced the king and the beggar, the extremes of wealth and poverty. "The great Æon" of "social lies that warp us from the living truth,"

"sinks in blood,

"And compass'd by the fires of Hell";

but the glorified friend, who looks at the tumult from the heights of divine vision, smiles, "*knowing* all is well," not merely believing it. And so would each of us, if we could reach those heights.

It would be hard to find a better commentary upon this passage than the closing words of *Progress and Poverty:* "Though Truth and Right seem often overborne, we may not see it all. How can we see it all? . . . Shall we say that what passes from our sight passes into oblivion? No; not into oblivion. Far, far beyond our ken the eternal laws must hold their sway.

"The hope that rises in the heart of all religions! The poets have sung it, the seers have told it, and in its deepest pulses the heart of man throbs responsive to its truth. This that Plutarch said is what in all times and in all tongues has been said by the pure-hearted and strong-sighted, who, standing, as it were, on the mountain-tops of thought and looking over the shadowy ocean, have beheld the loom of land :

"'Men's souls, encompass'd here with bodies and passions, have no communication with God, except what they can reach to in conception only, by means of philosophy as a kind of obscure dream. But, when they are loosed from the body and removed into the unseen, invisible, impassible, and pure region, this God is then their leader and king; they there, as it were, hanging on Him wholly, and beholding without weariness and passionately affecting that beauty which cannot be expressed or uttered by men.'"

What, then, is it that reconciles Understanding and Faith? What has enabled the poet to see the world of the Understanding through the eyes of Faith? It is Love, Love strong enough to conquer Death, and dispel his phantoms. In conquering Death, Love has taken away the prestige of the Understanding, which proclaims Death as the Lord of all things, and has handed over the victory to its weaker brother, "the lesser faith."[1] And victory in one point is victory

CXXVIII.

---

[1] But now abideth faith, hope, love, these three; and the greatest of these is love. — 1 Corinth xiii. 13.

in all. Faith, thus enthroned, is able to see
one consistent purpose in the universe. The
epochs of history are not merely so many aim-
less processions round the same weary race-
course, so many variations of an old theme
compounded of strife, delusion, schism, mum-
mery, revolution, pedantry, and sentimentality.[1]
If they were, they would deserve only scorn.
But, says the faith-enlightened poet,

> " I see in part
> That all, as in some piece of art,
> Is toil coöperant to an end."

This, then, if we may so speak, is the philosophical theory of *In Memoriam*. That higher
insight which we call faith, and upon which
we depend for the most vital truths, is feeble
when dissociated from love. Only through
love strong enough to burn away the last
shred of passion and, becoming purely spiritual, to lay hold upon the eternal in its object
can the power of the death-threatening understanding be subdued, and man become convinced that in the universe " all is well " forever, that his deepest and noblest aspirations
will find satisfaction in eternity. It is through
love that man rises to faith, and through faith
that he rises to God, " from whom is every

---

[1] One calls to mind here the saying of Hêrakleitos :
" The Æon is a child playing at draughts : to a child
belongs the sovereignty." (Frag., lxxix. edit. Bywater.)

good and perfect gift." This seems to be the
last word of all the great philosophical poems
of the world. It is the last word of that great
drama, the philosophical system of Plato;[1] it
is the last word of Dante's *Divine Comedy;*[2] it
is the last word of Goethe's *Faust;*[3] yea, it is
the last word of that great world-epic, the
Christian religion, as embodied in its true dis-
ciples.[4] It follows that the greatest loss which
can befall a human being is the loss of love.

Strong in love-begotten faith, the poet now
addresses his friend as an omnipres-
ent spirit, far off, yet near; known, CXXIX.
yet unknown; human, yet divine; dead, yet
immortal; lost, yet eternally his — " Mine,
mine forever, ever mine." He is now "loved
deeplier, darklier understood," loved most
when good is most clearly distinguished from
evil. Like Dante's Beatrice, he has become a
spiritual form for the divine itself, the form
suited to the poet's particular need.

> " Behold, I dream a dream of good,
> And mingle all the world with thee."

The divine loveliness takes as many forms as

[1] See *Lysis, Phaidros, Symposion,* etc.

[2] " Ma già volgeva il mio disiro e 'l velle,
  Sì come ruota che igualmente è mossa,
  L' Amor che muove il Sole e l'altre stelle."

[3] " Das Ewig-Weibliche
  Zieht uns hinan."

[4] He that loveth not knoweth not God; for God is
love. — 1 John, iv. 8.

there are hearts, and "he that loves not a brother whom he hath seen, cannot love God whom he hath not seen."

The lost one, now realized as having ascended from flesh to spirit,[1] from CXXX. space and time to infinity and eternity, is recognized as a diffusive power in the whole of nature, — not understood, but felt and loved deeply, darkly.

> "My love involves the love before;
>   My love is vaster passion now;
>   Tho' mix'd with God and Nature thou,
> I seem to love thee more and more."[2]

The poem closes with a prayer, than which there is nothing more nobly religious CXXXI. in all literature. It is addressed, not to any external God, but to the God within, to that "heaven-descended," "living Will," which is the essence of human personality, and which will endure

> "When all that seems shall suffer shock,"[3]

when the phenomenal world of sense shall be rolled up like a scroll. The poet calls upon it to rise, like a fountain, in the "spiritual rock," to "flow thro' our deeds and make them pure,"

---

[1] Dante, *Purg.*, xxx. 127.
[2] Compare Prologue, v. 10.

> "I trust he lives in thee, and there
> I find him worthier to be loved."

[3] Compare the poem entitled *Will*.

so that we may be able to rise above the mechanical world of dust, into a moral world of spirit, there to enter into conscious relations with the Infinite, the source of all life and action, and, through a faith born of self-control, may trust "the truths that never can be proved," until, in boundless love, we embrace, and become one with, the Absolute Love. Then we shall see

> "internalized,
> By Love into a single volume bound,
> All that is outered in the universe."[1]

Then all the powers of the spirit will be gathered into a

> "Light intellectual, filled full of love,
> Love of true good, filled full of joyfulness,
> A joyfulness transcending all things sweet."[2]

---

[1] Dante, *Parad.*, xxxiii. 85 *sqq.*

[2] *Ibid.*, xxx. 40 *sqq.* This verse was a favorite with Arthur Hallam. See his *Remains*, p. 145.

CHAPTER XVI.

Epilogue.

The New Life, full of joy and assurance. The Divine Process. Conclusion.

THE poet's moral world is now completely restored. He can act with assurance, as a man among men. He is happy. In this mood he celebrates the wedding of his sister Cecilia to Edmund Law Lushington, in a kind of Epithalamium, which forms an appropriate Epilogue to the poem. It is a picture of the New Life that has triumphed over death and doubt. Without it, the work would be incomplete. In the marriage of his sister the poet sees revealed that world-process by which Love lifts man out of sense and passion into spirituality and self-devotion — up to the measure of divine manhood, of which his friend was a type and an earnest. That friend now lives in God, who is life and love —

> " That God, which ever lives and loves,
> One God, one law, one element,
> And one far-off divine event,
> To which the whole creation moves."

Much might be said of these lines, which express the poet's view of what is deepest in the universe. By speaking of God as "which," he piously refrains from attributing to him personality in any form that would mean anything to us. No better commentary on this could be found than the following passage from Emerson's diary: "I say that I cannot find, when I explore my own consciousness, any truth in saying that God is a person, but the reverse. I feel that there is some profanation in saying that he is personal. To represent him as an individual is to shut him out of my consciousness. He is then but a great man, such as the crowd worships. The natural motions of the soul are so much better than the voluntary ones that you will never do yourself justice in dispute. The thought is not then taken hold of 'by the right handle'; does not show itself proportioned and in its true bearings. It bears extorted, hoarse, and half witness. I have been led, yesterday, into a rambling exculpatory talk on theism. I say that here we feel at once that we have no language; that words are only auxiliary and not adequate, are suggestions and not copies of our cogitation. I deny personality to God because it is too little, not too much. Life, personal life, is faint and cold to the energy of God. For Reason and Love and Beauty, or that which is all these, — it is the life of life, the reason of reason, the love of love." [1]

In speaking of God as Life, Law, Element, and End, the poet is a faithful disciple of Aristotle; for these are neither more nor less than that philosopher's four grounds or causes (αἰτίαι), without which nothing could exist at all. They are known familiarly as (1) the efficient cause, (2) the formal cause, (3) the material cause, and (4) the final cause. In the phenomenal world they are, or may be, sundered: in God they are united. The poet, moreover, follows his master in making life the fundamental cause. Aristotle says : "The energy of Mind (νοῦς) is life, and He is that energy. And self-energy is His best and eternal life. We say that God is living, eternal, best, so that life and an æon, perpetual and eternal, belong to God. For this is God." [2]

In this last verse of his poem the poet has taken a formal leave of the modern materialistic schools of thought dating from Locke, which deny the existence of teleology in the world, and has definitely ranged himself on the side of that spiritual philosophy which, since the days of Sôkratês, has accompanied and inspired the march of civilization, pointing out its goal. He stands with Sôkratês,

[1] Cabot's *Memoir of Ralph Waldo Emerson*, p. 341.
[2] *Metaph.*, xii. 7 : 1072*b* 26 *sqq.*

Plato, Aristotle, Philo, Plotinus, Porphyry, Thomas, Bonaventura, Rosmini; not with Locke, Hume, Kant, Fichte, Schelling, Hegel, Comte, Spencer. He holds that our life is from God to God, not from dirt to dirt, even though dirt be called Idea.

But in one point, and it is a most essential one, the poet goes beyond Aristotle, and includes in his God, yea, in the life of his God, an element which comes from Christian thought, and which is the fundamental characteristic of it — Love. The energy of the Christian god is not merely life; it is also and especially love. "God is Love." He is a god "which ever lives and *loves*." It is this addition that has given Christianity all its force and enabled it to transform the world: this, and this alone. It was, indeed, a wondrous new insight which could recognize that the very energy of life itself is love, that Love governs the world; that that which does not love is dead, however it may be galvanized into a semblance of life. As the late Professor Green puts it: "As the primary Christian idea is that of a moral death unto life, as wrought for us and in us by God, so its realization, which is the evidence of its truth, lies in Christian love — a realization never complete, because forever embracing new matter, yet constantly gaining in fulness."[1]

---

[1] *The Witness of God*, Works, vol. iii. pp. 236 *sq.*

It does not now seem difficult to sum up Tennyson's moral, life-shaping world-view: God is all in all, Life, Love, Law, Substance, End.   As Love, He is self-diffusive,[1] creating the world.   Human love is a manifestation of the divine love, a portion of that eternal energy forever working itself into a unitary, yet manifold, blessed self-consciousness, which is the

> "one far-off divine event
> To which the whole creation moves."

If we would be co-workers in this process, and share in its completion, we must, in self-sacrificing love, yield up our wills to the divine will.   In such self-sacrifice and "self-control" Faith will grow till it sees God, whom Love will then embrace and absorb.   Then the soul will feel and say to itself, "I and the Father are one."   "We must each become first a man, then a god."[2]   Through will we become the one; through love, the other.

---

[1] St. Bonaventura says finely : "*Bonum est diffusivum sui*" (Good is self-diffusive).

[2] Πρῶτον οὖν ἄνθρωπον δεῖ γενέσθαι, τότε δὲ θεόν. Hieroklês, Commentary to *The Golden Verses.*

INDEX TO IN MEMORIAM.

INDEX TO IN MEMORIAM.

R.

RACE (*running*)

9.	5.	my widow'd *r.*
17.	5.	my widow'd *r.*
42.	1.	outstript me in the *r.*
114.	4.	in her onward *r.*

RACE (*generation*)

74.	1.	to some one of his *r.*
102.	1.	one of stranger *r.*
103.	9.	great *r.* which is to be
118.	4.	herald of a higher *r.*
123.	2.	*races* may degrade
Ep.	32.	the crowning *r.*

RAGE

27.	1.	void of noble *r.*

RAIN

7.	3.	the drizzling *r.*
98.	8.	in emerald *r.*

RANGE

93.	3.	thy sightless *r.*

RANK

60.	1.	*r.* exceeds her own
103.	6.	*ranks* Of iris
111.	1.	the scale of *ranks*

RAPT (*verb*)

103.	13.	So *r.* I was

RAVINE

56.	4.	With *r.*

REACH

71.	4.	the river's wooded *r.*

REALM

40.	3.	*realms* of love

REASON

33.	4.	countest *r.* ripe
61.	1.	*r.* change replies
112.	2.	art *r.* why
124.	4.	*reason's* colder part

RECORD

31.	2.	lives no *r.* of reply
52.	3.	What *r.* ?

RED (*adj.*)

99.	2.	thro' thy darkling *r.*

REDRESS

106.	3.	*r.* to all mankind

REED

84.	12.	What *r.* was that
100.	2.	whispering *r.*
103.	6.	golden *r.*

REEF

36.	4.	round the coral *r.*

REFLEX

108.	3.	*r.* of a human face

REFRACTION

92.	4.	*r.* of events

REGION

78.	2.	No wing of wind the *r.* swept

REGRET

8.	5.	my deep *r.*
29.	1.	chains *r.* to his decease
40.	2.	light *regrets*
78.	5.	O last *r.*, *r.* can die
102.	6.	one pure image of *r.*
115.	5.	*r.* Becomes
116.	1.	*r.* for buried time
116.	3.	Not all *r.*
Ep.	4.	a dead *r.*
Ep.	5.	*R.* is dead

REJOICE (*verb*)

130.	4.	I *r.* ; I prosper

RELATION

78.	5.	Her deep *relations*

RELIC

17.	5.	precious *relics*

RELIEF

24.	3.	sets the past in this *r.*
85.	2.	so to bring *r.*

REPLY (*verb*)

103.	13.	but he *Replying*

REPORT

14.	1.	bring me this *r.*

REPROACH

85.	4.	Thro' light *reproaches*

REST (*repose*)

11.	5.	sway themselves in *r.*
27.	3.	want-begotten *r.*
30.	5.	surely *r.* is meet
67.	1.	thy place of *r.*
104.	2.	this hour of *r.*

REST (*remainder*)

31.	4.	*r.* remaineth unreveal'd
Ep.	22.	perchance among the *r.*

RESULT

1.	4.	the long *r.* of love
73.	4.	the large *results* Of force

www.ingramcontent.com/pod-product-compliance
Lightning Source LLC
Chambersburg PA
CBHW031110020726
47495CB00007B/2136